BIKER

Short Stories

DELARISTO STILLGESS

authorHOUSE®

AuthorHouse™
1663 Liberty Drive
Bloomington, IN 47403
www.authorhouse.com
Phone: 1 (800) 839-8640

Published by AuthorHouse   02/27/2018

ISBN: 978-1-5462-2804-2 (sc)
ISBN: 978-1-5462-2803-5 (e)

Print information available on the last page.

Any people depicted in stock imagery provided by Getty Images are models, and such images are being used for illustrative purposes only. Certain stock imagery © Getty Images.

This book is printed on acid-free paper.

Because of the dynamic nature of the Internet, any web addresses or links contained in this book may have changed since publication and may no longer be valid. The views expressed in this work are solely those of the author and do not necessarily reflect the views of the publisher, and the publisher hereby disclaims any responsibility for them.

CONTENTS

Motorcycles
Rust or Ride
Ride or Rust

Motorcycles
Dusk to Dawn
Dawn to Dusk

Delaristo Stillgess

My pride and joy

A LIFE CHANGING TRIP

It was a cold and snowy day in November. The day before Thanksgiving. Discouraged, depressed, displaced and depleted, I made a decision that would change my life forever. I reluctantly sold one caddy and gave the other to my daughter, and gave my much loved and well trained Doberman, named Brandy, to a total stranger. That is an indication of just how depressed I was. But the biggest state of depression that I felt crushed my heart, was yet to happen.

Reluctantly and sadly, with a heavy heart, I got down on my knees and hugged my children as I told them that I was going away. I had every intention to return as soon as I could get a good job and could financially make our lives better. To me, it was heartbreaking because I don't think they could quite understand or grasp the idea that things happen in life. That we don't want or don't want to face. At any rate, I knew that I had to do something to better my life so that I could better their lives even if it meant going to another state and changing my environment. I felt so closed in, as if the world was closing in around me.

My best friends were not my friends anymore. I was getting stabbed in the back over and over again by people whom I trusted with all my heart. I just couldn't take it anymore. I did a year in the state prison for something I did not do, which damaged my reputation and lost even more friends. Before I was locked down from the freedom of life as I knew it, I was told that I was the father of a baby boy whom I actually named at first, but when I came back from prison, I'm told that he was not my son. I was devastated.

I just had to get away.

I had no idea that the time would go by so fast. Months turned in to years and before I knew it, my kids were turning into adults. I tried to stay in contact with them throughout the years by communication on holidays, birthdays, and even drove alone on road trips from Houston, Texas, to be sure to visit my children on Christmas Eve.

As time passed, my visits became far more less frequent. Life has a way of changing your plans. You can't always do what you plan to do, even though you have the best intentions. So for now, I'll leave that right there. I decided to, in my mind, rid all of my troubles and problems by just getting on my bike (motorcycle) and let the wind hit me in the face.

I didn't want to take the normal route to California because that route was already covered with snow in some states. Imagine me riding my motorcycle on highways that had up to six feet of snow. So I decided to take the

Southern route and try to beat the winter storms. Even though it was a longer way, more miles, I was going to try.

I remember when I stopped at a gas station in Kentucky for gas and a hot coffee, I was surprised to see a group of four white men were standing around my bike, looking at it. My first thought was, "oh-oh, trouble." Being in the hills of Kentucky where it has been said to be racist, I immediately put up my guard. But as I walked closer to my bike, they greeted me with smiles and reached out to shake my hand, referring to my "Ohio" license plate (which was Coole), and saying "we knew you Buckeyes were "badass" but we didn't know you were this badass," referring to me riding a motorcycle across country with six inches of snow already on the ground.

They wished me well as I continued my journey.

I slipped and slided on the snow and ice and about lost it several times. My speed limit was held down to no more than ten miles an hour. Cars and 18 wheelers were speeding past me and it took every ounce of energy for me to hold my two wheels up, so as not to fall over.

I finally out ran the snow storm as I got further down south.

I reached and by-passed New Orleans and finally got to highway 10 west. From there it was a straight shot west to California. It hadn't snowed here but it was very cold. The road was clear and the morning sun felt very good, providing heat. I was now on the super highway and making good time.

I noticed there were not any cars passing me nor were there any cars on the side of the road. No oncoming traffic at all. I wondered why I was the only one on the what normally be a traffic filled highway. I finally figured it out and the answers to my questions were now plain to see. As I looked into my rear view mirror, I could see dark skies and a dark, twisting funnel rapidly approaching. It was an amazingly beautiful tornado just a few miles behind me and coming my way. Oh my God, I said to myself. I saw an overpass a few miles ahead and I drove up to 115 miles an hour to get there.

I hopped off of the bike and laid down and wedged my body between the roof and the stone of the underpass and as I looked up, it was now going down the road ahead of me. I was in somewhat of a shock and disbelief. I just outran and survived a tornado.

I can live through anything now, I thought to myself, as I got on my bike and continued to my destination.

I was now riding about 80 miles an hour to make up for lost time.

It was now Thanksgiving day.

Once I arrived in Texas and crossed the state line, it seemed like hours before I came to a Texas city to gas up again. I came to a city called Beaumont and while at the gas station, I noticed a fine honey checking me out. She asked me where I was from and where I was going. We exchanged formalities and she told me to stick around for at least an half-hour and she would get me a room at the Motel 6 so I could rest awhile. Call me in thirty minutes, she said, as she put her digits in my hand along with three brand new crisp twenty dollar bills.

Just as she did that, a nice lookin, muscular, well dressed guy came out of the gas station and started pumping gas in her new BMW. Then he got in the car and when they shared a kiss, I wasn't about to get caught up in some crap over a disloyal, beautiful woman. Pleased that I now had an extra 60 in my pocket, I was in the road again. Next stop – Houston, Texas.

In two and a half hours, I was now in Houston. It was around 9 a.m. I stopped at a gas station to refill gas and coffee. I pulled up to the front door so as to drink some coffee before getting the gas.

While I sat on my bike resting, I watched a guy pull up to the gas pumps on a nice, fully-dressed Honda Gold Wing. As he was getting his gas, two more guys pulled up to him and I could tell they were not his friends. They were yelling back and forth at each other and suddenly the two bikers pulled off the guy's leather vest and threw it on the ground and stomped on it. Then to my astonishment, one of the evil bikers pulled out his dick and pissed all over it. I sat there in disbelief at what I just witnessed. Suddenly, the two bold bikers started walking over to me. I said to myself, "oh shit, I'll be damn if I let them piss on my jacket. As the two Latino bikers come up to me. One guy stands in front of my bike while the other stands right beside me. I had already placed my hand inside my vest pocket, my fingers tickling my ivory handled .38 pistol.

The guy beside me seemed to be the brains of them both, for he did all the talking.

He looked at my Ohio license tags and asked me if I had paid my toll. I said that I didn't know anything about any toll. He replied, "Oh yeah, you have to pay a forty dollar toll to ride your bike through here. Suddenly, the guy in front of me put his hands on my windshield and I started praying to God in silence to myself, please God don't let me have to shoot these men, please, God!

I stared into the eyes of the guy standing to the left of me with a hard, mean, cold stare and I said, "Look man, I have been riding all night and I am sleepy, hungry, and tired as hell. I don't care if I have to sleep in a jail cell. If you don't tell this mutherfucker to take his hands off my bike, I'm going to jail and you both are going to the hospital." We stared at each other for what seemed like an eternity. But in reality, it was just a few minutes. He told his partner to back off. "He's ok," he said, as they walked backwards towards their bikes parked at the gas pumps.

I said, "Thank you, Jesus" as the two outlaw bikers mounted on their older Harley's and rode away.

I was so shaken from this encounter that I didn't even go into the station for a cup of coffee or get gas. I decided to get out of there in case the troublemakers changed their minds and came back.

As I was riding down the S.W. freeway, also known as Highway 59, I was so tired that I decided to get off the freeway and ride along the feeder. I happened to see an old dilapidated hotel. The windows and doors were boarded up and broken concrete steps were surrounded by four foot tall weeds.

As I slowly rode by, I noticed in front of the hotel was a tent made of cardboard boxes and I could see someone laying inside it. I rode on for about another mile or so, and I thought to myself, "I bet that guy was hungry." I know I was hungry! I thought to myself, "since this is Thanksgiving, I'm going to go back and give thanks with that homeless man."

So I pulled over and gassed up the bike, bought a rotisserie chicken, loaf of bread, and two 40 ounces of Schlitz Malt Liquor, took it back to the homeless man and as his feet was sticking out from the cardboard boxes, I nudged them and told him it's time to wake up and let's eat. This homeless man was about eighty-two years old. A small framed, 5'2" dark brown skinned and the whitest full head of hair that accented his dark brown complexion.

He was such a pleasant man and very soft spoken. He spoke of how all nine of his adult children had turned their backs on him. He fell on hard times and no one seemed to care. We spent an hour or so talking as he ate. I lost my appetite and told him to eat the chicken and bread but I did manage to drink the malt liquor. Well, I bid my new friend a farewell and thought I'd get on down the road.

I rode another twenty miles and it dawned on me that I knew someone that lived here in Houston. I just happened to have the phone number of a childhood friend that has always been like a little brother to me. Shout out to Robert Finch, aka, Bob Slim.

When he answered the phone, I automatically knew his voice and said, "Guess who's coming to dinner?" We both laughed and I must say it was a pleasure to hear his voice after all these years. I was invited to his house and he and his family greeted me with open arms. I was treated to a great Thanksgiving dinner and, believe me, I was truly thankful. I was amazed of how ten year old Jabari was well trained in his father's auto detailing business.

Well, after spending the night and resting, Bob Slim offered me a detailing job, and because that was my profession, I accepted. The rest is history. I never made it to California.

As I regress, it was Thanksgiving day and Bob Slim and his significant other, Malika, and their son Jabari made me feel right at home, with the hospitality that would make any king feel at ease.

I was invited to stay at their residence. Bob Slim offered me a job and a place to lay my head. It all sounded good to me since I was really tired anyway, and the rest of the road to Southern California seemed so long to travel to now.

So I hunkered down and when I saved enough money to get my own apartment, I moved into it. I didn't have any furniture but I did manage to get a king size bed from an auction of a hotel.

It was a hot, muggy Friday night in March. I jumped on my bike and rode to the South Side of Houston where it was known to have Biker clubs in the predominantly Black or African American neighborhoods.

The first club that I went to was very interesting. It was called The Golden Eagles Motorcycle Club. When I first pulled into the parking lot, I couldn't help but notice the three long rows of neatly parked, beautiful motorcycles. Mostly Harley Davidsons. All shape, sizes, and colors. I parked my Harley Road King as close to the entrance as possible.

As I was walking through the door, I was abruptly bumped into by two large muscular men whom were fighting. The first acts of physical violence that I've seen in a long time. And it was right there just an arm's length away. Well, in the fracas, the dueling men pushed up against me for the second time, so feeling threatened, I pushed them both from me. They fell but continued to fight and as a result all three of us was kicked out of the club.

Can you believe that crap? Here I am, minding my own business and get kicked out before I could even get a cold beer.

I continued on to find a cool place to party and hang out with some cool people. Little did I know but I was in the most roughest and most dangerous neighborhood in Houston,Third Ward. I was riding down Hiram Creek Boulevard and passed a club that had at least 100 motorcycles parked and seemed like several hundred people just congregating. I made a u-turn and quickly found my spot among a crowd of people and did not know a single person. I made my way to the bar and finally a nice ice cold 40 oz. was the object of my attention. It was a chilled and relaxing atmosphere even though I didn't know one single person.

As I mingled through the crowd, suddenly I heard a roar of thundering motorcycles pulling in off the street. It was 8 to 10 bikers that their very presence demanded respect from everyone. I didn't know who these brothers were but I know I liked their style. They parked in a corner of the lot and seemed to stay to themselves, even though several people showed respect by speaking and talking to them.

I walked up and introduced myself to the first brother I came to. His name was Roy Norman, better known as Storm. An ex-marine of twenty years, he proved to become a very close friend. Next I met Raleigh Jackson, aka Tracker. A deputy sheriff, he also became one of the coolest people I know. Then came Donald Jackson, aka, DJ- no relation to tracker but just as cool. These turned into be my running buddies and we formed a brothership/bond and had each others' backs. Then, of course, there was "Boot Scooter," Pit Bull, and several others that was in our group. We called ourselves the P's Motorcycle Club. We became well known among the hot motorcycle clubs in all of Houston. I might say very well respected among most men, envied by others. We were very popular and respected by the women-folk, if I must say so myself. We had several clubs that we would frequent on certain nights of the week. And we never had to pay a cover charge to get in like others did.

Those were the days.

I told my life-long friends Albert Porter, Richard Trent, and George Webster that I was going to ride my Harley to Ohio to visit. I was so surprised and happy when Albert and George rode to Houston so that I would have someone to ride to Ohio with. I was disappointed that Richard didn't come but I sure was glad to see my other brothers. I took them to Sunny Side, another rough and dangerous part of the city, so they could meet my biker family. We, along with fifteen other bikers, bar hopped to four of our favorite bars until ending the night at 4 a.m. at my favorite place.

When we arrived to the house it was funny because Albert said, "Oh my God! I just put 75 miles on the speedometer and we never even left the city.

We got a good nights sleep. The next day we bar-b-que'd, then jumped on the bikes and started bar hopping all over again.

Unfortunately, in recent years my good friends Storm and D.J. both lost their battles with cancer. R.I.P. Roy Norman and Donald Jackson. We miss you!

Later, I found out that I had a cousin in Houston, also. Shout out to Darren Roberts and family.

As time passed, I became familiar with the bikers and biker clubs in Houston. Every Friday and Saturday the bikers would be out in force. But Sunday was my special day. Bikers from all over Houston would meet and greet on Reed Road. That's where I met some of the coolest people that I know. We formed a club called the "P's." Shout out to the P's. Shout out to the "Tracker" Raleigh Jackson and his wife, Amy. I know you are Tru-Cons now. Shout out to the Tru-Cons. Keep the rubber side down! Keep the rubber on the road!

Inga "Pit Bull" Johnson of Houston, Texas

Albert "AP" Porter of Dayton, Ohio

A TRUE ROAD TALE
(A 2-ply Lesson for All "Bikers")

I just want to bring this to the attention of all bikers, no matter what age or nationality you may be. We as bikers, be it every day riders or weekend warriors, we need to "look out" for one another. We all have one thing for sure in common. We love to ride, work on, customize to our individual tastes, and take great pride in our motorcycles. Our bikes are an extension of our personalities.

I've been riding now going on fifty-two years and I have learned to respect the power, the road, and other drivers at an early age. I have had my share of spills and highway breakdowns. I can remember one time I was riding my Gold Wing from California to Vegas. I was anxious to get there and with the hustle and bustle and the excitement of taking my new lady friend to spend our first romantic weekend together, I forgot to do one of the most important things. I forgot to fill-up the gas tank! Duh!!

There we were, eleven-thirty at night, cruising down Highway 15, in the middle of the desert. The cassette was playing my favorite jazz tunes. My lady was singing along and enjoying the ride while massaging my shoulders. I felt like I was in motorcycle-ridin' heaven. Big ol' smile on my face. I just happened to look down at the gauge and noticed that the gas tank was not even up to "E." We must have been riding on fumes. I turned on the reserve tank and sighed a sigh of relief. The relief didn't last long, though. We were crossing the desert and there was nothing in sight for as far as we could see. No lights or signs of human life anywhere.

By the time the gas gauge reached "E," I decided to pull over to avoid going completely empty. Needless to say, but I felt I was dumber than dumb. I felt so stupid that I had to laugh at myself to keep from crying. I was fortunate that I had a lady friend that could laugh along with me instead of giving me a hard time about it. Several cars went by and no one offered to stop and give aid. Some of them even had the nerve to honk their horn and wave as they drove by.

Going on three hours later, seemed liked hundreds of cars had passed us. Suddenly, from a far off distance, I could hear the familiar beautiful rumble of motorcycles. As they drew nearer, the headlights of several "bikes" became brighter and brighter. Suddenly, a dozen bikes passed us and man I mean to tell you they were rollin'. They were nothing but a big blur. My heart sang!

"Oh, yes!" I yelled with excitement. "Look honey – they are pulling over." They were about five or six miles down the road but I could see all of the tail lights and they had come to a complete stop. A few minutes went by and all of a sudden one single headlight left the bunch and was now speeding towards us. As the rider pulled up on a beautiful "Fat Boy" he asked if we were having trouble. Feeling totally stupid and helpless, I told him of our plight. He then assured me it was alright and he pulled away. When he reached his comrades, they pulled away and the ground seemed to shake as the roar of the bikes sounded like thunder.

An hour had passed and it was now after four in the morning. Suddenly, in the distance here come five headlights. When they pulled up to us, an older gentleman with a kind face and warm smile, probably in his middle 70's, handed me a four gallon can of gasoline. I was so happy that I gave that ol' man a big hug, ha, ha, ha, and we all busted out in laughter.

We all rode on to Vegas together!

The moral of this story is a 2-ply learning experience. Always make sure you have a full tank of gas and always take time to stop and help our fellow biker! No matter what creed or color! We all need to stick together!

Kenneth "Barron" Seelig with his wife
Staci of Springfield, Ohio

Deputy Raleigh "Tracker" Jackson, and
his wife Amy of Houston, Texas

TEEN CHOP SHOP

Awakening to the alarm clock at 6:30 in the morning to the sounds of Marvin Gaye's, "Let's Get It On," automatically put me in a mellow mood. I could hardly sleep the night before because I knew the next day, which is today, I would be purchasing the very thing I've been avoiding to purchase for years – a brand new Harley Davidson Road King.

The reason why I say "avoiding to purchase" is because back in the day I was skeptical of buying a Harley because of the many rumors that I heard about them. Such as, they break down all the time, or every time you ride one for 100 miles or so you have to stop and tighten up all the nuts and bolts, and plus, they were so expensive, one would have to sell an arm and a leg to afford one. But, in spite of all these rumors, deep down inside I still wanted one. I've come to realize that this was my missing link. I had heard that with the modern day technology, the Harley is made better, runs better, looks better, and is a much sturdier bike. So today is my big day! I'm going to purchase my first Harley and I'm so excited.

Now I've had several bikes in my fifty-two years of riding including two Honda Gold Wings, an 1100 Suzuki, a 900 Kawasaki, two 1100 Honda Shadows, and I'll never forget my first bike, a 750 Honda. They were all beautiful and very well kept but I still felt a void in my life. Something was missing! After all these years of being on the biker scene and participating in biker parties and functions from New York to California, I still needed something to fill the overwhelming void.

As I walk through the showroom, across the room I see a beautiful, luscious red Road King, white walls and all. That's my baby right there, I said to myself. I added a few accessories and within a few hours I was pulling out onto the feeder road along the Southwest freeway, Big ol' smile on my face! Yes indeed I was smilin' like a chessy cat! I rode all over town and believe me, I was a happy camper. Nothing could spoil my day! Nothing!

While cruising, visions of myself on my new Harley could be seen in the store-front windows as I passed by, making me realize that I finally filled that empty void in my life. I finally reached that ultimate goal! I finally owned a brand spankin' new Harley Davidson. (Well, me and the finance company) (smiles), but I'm the one who's ridin' it – ha ha!

I pulled into a restaurant to get something to eat and I made sure that I parked the bike in front of the window so I could marvel at it while having lunch. I decided to treat myself since this is a special day. I ordered the largest T-bone steak in the house with all the trimmings. I noticed that several people would walk up to my bike and gaze at it. I also spotted a few cars driving by slowly as the people pointed and stared at it. It made me feel good that so many people were admiring my bike. I must admit, she was a beautiful sight with all that shiny chrome.

Well, I finished eating and decided to hit the "little boy's room" before I hit the road. As I washed my hands and looked into the mirror, I smiled at myself and said, "you lucky dawg, you!"

Suddenly there was a knock on the restroom door and a lady's voice said, "excuse me sir, but did you call someone to pick up your bike?" I opened the door and said, "H--- No!" She then said, "well somebody is taking it!" A feeling of sheer panic and confusion entered my body as I ran out the door. I could see my precious Harley in the back of a pick-up truck pulling away from the parking lot. I panicked! Rage swelled in my soul!

I saw a man getting into an old tore up Volkswagon Bug, about a 1970 or so. I asked him to follow that truck but he said he couldn't do it. Getting more and more upset and frustrated by the second, I yelled at this completely total stranger and told him to get out of his car. I jumped in the driver's seat and took off in chase. I looked in the rearview mirror and seeing the stranger standing there, I realized – "Hey ---What am I doing?" So, I backed up – yelled for him to get in – he did!

In pursuit of my "baby" on it, I pushed that little Volkswagon for all it was worth. Jumping in and out of lanes and nearly side-swiping several cars, I was determined to get my "baby" back. I followed the truck through several neighborhoods and it finally pulled into a large garage with the overhead door closing behind it.

I cautiously made my way to a window and peeked in. There to my surprise was a whole room full of Harley's and Corvettes. There were several young boys between the ages of 12 to 15 years old, taking parts off of the bikes. As I watched, I felt a pressure of cold steel on the back of my head. "Don't move" a young voice said. I was then pushed inside the garage and immediately surrounded by a gang of kids, all holding guns on me. A little fat kid who seemed to be the ring leader stuck a chrome-plated pistol in my mouth and said, "we have no choice now – we must kill him!" As I started praying to my Father God, I felt a tug on my foot and a voice saying – WAKE UP! WAKE UP! WAKE UP!

I suddenly sat up in the bed and realized that I was only dreaming. "Oh my Lord, Thank you Jesus," I said as I got up to start my day. I guess I'll go out into the garage and fire up my baby. (smile)

Row of motorcycles

Compliments of Wayne and Avonda May

"HONEY, THIS HARLEY IS FOR YOU!"

My! My! My! I am so glad to finally get out of that truck so I can breathe and stretch my legs. I don't know how long I've been in there. I've lost all sense of time. All I can say is that I'm so happy to be here in this beautiful place with all of my new friends. Today is my first day in this place and I can't wait to see if I'm going to be taken out for a cool spin around town.

As I sit here mesmerized, I hear the jingling of keys at the front door. "Who is it?" I wonder to myself. Suddenly the darkness is chased away with light. I can hear someone whistling but I don't see anyone! Um um um, I smell the pleasant aroma of coffee brewing.

Footsteps! I hear many footsteps! There must be at least seven or eight different patterns of sounds of boots clomping in the near distance. Suddenly I can hear the footsteps coming closer and closer to me. There she is! A small lady with tiny feet, about five feet tall with long red shoulder length hair starts rubbing my shoulders with something nice and cool – a soft towel. It feels so good! This is so great! She is making me feel right at home, teasing and tickling me with her tantalizing fingers. ALLLLLL OVERRRRR MY BODYYYYY! Man, this sure feels good!

As she finishes with me, I notice she is doing the same rub-downs to my friends across the room. Well, I guess I'll relax and enjoy my day.

I've been here for several hours now and a total of eleven people have come to visit me. It seems that everyone looks at me with smiles on their faces and love in their hearts. It's so nice to be loved by total strangers. As different people gaze at me then walk away, I noticed that the same man keeps walking around me and staring at me. Now he's bringing another guy over to me. I can barely hear what they are saying but I can tell that they are talking about me. It must be something nice because they both are smiling.

All of a sudden, one of the guys from another room comes and takes me outside. We cruise a few miles then it's back to the same spot. The two men talk again but this time I can hear the one guy say, "Yes, my wife is going to love it." I wonder if the "it" he's talking about is me? Well, I'll know soon enough!

They pick me up into a trailer and I'm thinking to myself that I really don't want to go with this man but I'll go just to get out and enjoy the fresh air and open road. We travel several miles and I can't help but to be curious as to where I am going.

The Chevy truck finally pulls into a drive-way and I wait patiently while he goes inside the house. A few minutes later, the big man comes out with a beautiful young lady and as she is grinning from ear to ear, she straddles on my back and I hear the kind man say, "Happy birthday, honey. This Harley is for you!"

Bikers ready to roll!

Delaristo "Bus Coole" Stillgess

FIVE FOOT FOUR

There were two warring motorcycle clubs: one that lived in the big city, and the other in a small country town. The big city bikers were a group of violent, disrespecting, drug dealing no-goods. They were known for hijacking other unsuspecting bikers for their new Harley's and Honda's by using brute force and, of course, by gunpoint.

The country town "riders" consisted of five hard-working, respectful, down to earth Christians. They all had the same thing in common – they loved to ride their motorcycles on the weekends. The big city bikers invaded the country town bikers. One day, and as part of their plundering of the people, they hijacked one of the Harley's and took it back to the big city.

The country town fellas didn't know anything about the big city. They didn't know where to look in the over crowded neighborhoods and they had no clue where to start. They received very little help from the law enforcers, who stated that "this sort of thing happens every day – no big deal." Even so, the small town boys sent everyone they could think of to the big city to find the stolen motorcycle. They sent the police, the FBI, the CIA, and even bounty hunters.

They visited motorcycle clubs all over the city, from one clubhouse to another. After several days of effort, checking every back alley, every chop shop known of, and every violent, ruthless neighborhood, they still came up empty-handed. Feeling hopeless and helpless, the country town men decided that the cause was lost, and they prepared to return to the quiet hills of the country.

As they were packing their gear to leave, they saw the stolen Harley's' 5'4", 120 pound female owner coming up the street towards them in her bright yellow Hummer vehicle. They realized that she was pulling a motorcycle trailer, and lo and behold, her stolen Harley was on the trailer.

How could that be?

One man greeted her and said, "We couldn't find your Harley. How did you do this when we, the biggest, strongest, bravest, and most able men from our small country town couldn't do it?"

She shrugged her shoulders and said, "It wasn't your Harley!"

The moral of the story: Where there's a will, there's a way. If you love something or somebody enough, you'll find a way!

Deputy Raleigh "Tracker" Jackson and his wife, Amy.

Rick Seelig and friends

HARLEY DAVIDSON EMBLEM (POWERFUL COLORS)

I woke up this morning with one thing heavy on my mind. I need to get to the library so I can use the computer to type my three short stories. It bothered me all night that my own computer was on the blink, and to top it off, my Road King was down (water and rust in the gas tank). Also, my Harley truck was stolen over the weekend. So, if I didn't have bad luck, I wouldn't have any luck at all.

Since I had so many problems on my mind and I really didn't have anything else to do, I decided to be adventurous and walk the seven mile hike to the nearest library. The exercise would do me good and the long walk would give me some time alone to think and hash out my problems.

Out of habit, I throw on some Harley jeans, a sweat shirt, my most comfortable pair of Harley boots, my black and orange Harley jacket, and I wouldn't feel complete without my Harley skull cap. As I walked out the door, I noticed the sky was so beautiful. "Such a good day to take a long walk," I thought to myself as I approached the third block from my house. With two more blocks to go,

I'll be on highway seventy-three, turn left, and begin the seven mile trek.

As I take my first step on the highway, I'm singing to myself and feeling happy already. Why am I so happy? Lord only knows, I guess it's because even though I'm not on my bike, I'm still feeling the freedom of being out on the open road.

While walking, the first mile or so felt really good. Then it hit me! Man, I thought I'd fall out! My comfortable boots were not so comfortable anymore. My legs were getting weary but I thought to myself that I had come this far I may as well keep going. By the time I was into the fourth mile I was really tired but I remembered how just last summer I rode my bike from Texas to Ohio and every time I would get tired, I would repeat to myself, "Determination will get me across the nation." Over and over I would say this just to keep me from falling asleep. So I repeated it to myself as I walked down the highway.

Look at my Harley timepiece, two and a half hours has passed and I have about one mile or so to go. I've already stepped over "roadkill." So far I've seen four snakes, four rats, two dogs, one huge snapping turtle, two very large bullfrogs, and one armadillo – all of this on this little stretch of highway. It would take a lot to get me out here walking at night. If I came face to face with those critters after dark, I would really freak out. I'd probably be running the whole way. It's my assumption that they were probably alive during the darkness until their untimely demise.

I have a habit of looking down while walking and sometimes it pays off. I found a total of two quarters, three dimes, one nickel, and seven pennies. Makes me wonder! Do people actually throw money out of their windows? How else would money be on the side of the highway? Some of it looked as if it's been there a long time. "Well, I'll put it back into circulation," I said to myself.

Suddenly, I see a white SUV backing up towards me. "Who is this," I wondered? As I opened the door, to my surprise it was my friend Joyce. "What the heck are you doing walking way out here?" she asked, as I entered the vehicle. "I'm on a mission to type my stories at the library," I replied. As she dropped me off at the library, and upon entering the building, it began to rain. Feeling tired and worn out, I was glad to be able to sit down at a computer. I didn't want to think about the rain. Finally, when I finished my work, I started the long walk back, only this time it was raining cats and dogs.

While walking along the feeder road, the first two cars passed and splashed water all over me. I was soaking wet before I even got to the highway. Another penny, another dead snake, another mile, another armadillo, another dead dog. No, wait a minute! That's not a dog! That's a coyote or maybe a wolf. It's definitely not a dog! I stand there and stare inquisitively for a minute. The rain continued to soak me even more.

I walk another two miles and every car or eighteen-wheeler that passes me does its share of splashing water on me. My feet are getting cold! My nose is sniffing! My legs and lower back are stiff and sore at the same time.

With each step I take, I feel like there are weights in my boots. I'm feeling miserable and yearn to get home to get out of these wet clothes. I've got a big hot cup of coffee on my mind!

Suddenly, a truck pulls up beside me a total stranger waves for me to get in. Surprised and elated, I opened the door. The first thing I see is the Harley Davidson emblem on the dashboard and Harley Davidson seat covers. The steering wheel is even covered with the emblem. I immediately felt comfortable with the stranger because I knew we had something in common, our love for the Harley.

He took me the last four miles and that really made my day. As soon as I get out of these clothes, dry myself off and have a coffee, I'm going to send my stories out and pray that someone can use them. It's been a good but wet day and my spirit is happy.

Alex "Doc" Gross, Jr.; Raleigh "Tracker"
Jackson; and Roy "Storm" Norman

The P's

Left to Right:
Kenneth "Pay Less" Paley; Raleigh "Tracker" Jackson;
Donald "DJ" Jackson; Roy "Storm" Norman; Rudolph
"Rudy D" Davis; Terrence Norman; Delaristo "Bus
Coole" Stillgess; Terrence "Nighthawk" Hubbard.

EVERYBODY IS NOT A BIKER

It was a bright, sunny, beautiful day in May. The sky was filled with gorgeous, fluffy white clouds, scattered in various patterns as far as the eye could see. The softness of silence covered the rolling hills of clover like a blanket, but the sounds of mother nature blended in harmony like the most beautiful ballad. Birds sang in unfamiliar tunes. Bees buzzed louder than usual. An occasional frog could be heard croaking his part in nature's ensemble. Even the barking of a dog from a far-off distance made the day seem so peaceful.

I strolled down to the creek and dangled my toes in the clear cool waters. I sat there for hours under the gigantic weeping willow tree and day dreamed. As I sat there and swatted at pesky insects, I could look both ways down the country road. No heavy traffic in sight! An occasional tractor and maybe an eighteen wheeler would pass by. Suddenly, the ground started trembling! The birds stopped singing! Even the bees all seemed to leave the glorious flowers and zoom out of sight. I noticed the frogs stopped croaking and began to scurry out of eye's view. What could be the matter, I thought to myself. I pulled out my binoculars and gazed at both ends of the road but still there was nothing coming or going.

The earth shook and trembled again!

I climbed as high as I could in a nearby weeping willow so I could get a better view. "What the heck is that," I whispered to myself in disbelief. Far off was a bright shiny glare that seemed to be moving through the winding hill like a snake covered with glistening diamonds. As my heart started beating double time, I could feel the excitement growing in my veins. I still didn't know exactly what I was witnessing. Suddenly, the sounds of a rumble, a deep rumble, move like a roar of a den of lions filled the air. Louder and louder it became! The shiny snake-like figures became more visible now. Within in seconds – there it was!

To my surprise, one of the most prettiest sights I've ever seen. One, two, three, four, five – seventy, eighty, ninety – one-hundred. Oh my goodness, there are too many to count. More and more, riding in sets of two's. The most beautiful motorcycles I've ever laid eyes on. Big shiny chrome-filled bikes with men and women of all colors, riding on the bikes of all colors. The roar of the bikes was now like thunder and it sounded like music to my ears. As the long bearded and the clean shaven, leather wearin' bikers rode past me, they seemed to be very friendly because they all waved and some even blew their horns at me. I could sense the friendliness!

As the last bikes went by, the very last bike had a big American flag on it. I have never seen the flag look so grand! My curiosity grew wider! Who were they? Where did they come from? Where were they going? They looked as if they were having so much fun! I wish I were riding with them. And now – silence again!

The frogs are back sitting on the rocks. The bees are dancing with the flowers! The birds are singing joyously! I'm going back to feeding chickens and the pigs but I have to admit, for a few minutes I felt overwhelming pure excitement in my life.

The moral of this story: Everybody is not a biker – but they wish they were!

Top row, left to Right: Raleigh "Tracker" Jackson and his wife Amy; Henry "Boots Scooter" Jackson Bottom row, left to Right: Roy "Storm" Norman; Donald "DJ" Jackson; Delaristo "Bus Coole" Stillgess.

The Black Diamonds MCC
Urbana, Ohio

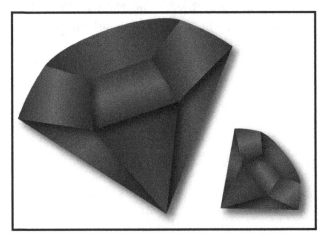

Black Diamonds

A LESSON LEARNED THE HARD WAY (PLEASE! PLEASE! PLEASE!)

If you are a diabetic and you ride a "bike" or drive a vehicle, please, please, please take very good care of yourself and your diabetic situation.

I am a diabetic, diagnosed in 1999 and sometimes I feel so healthy that I forget to keep a close concern on controlling diabetes. Diabetes Type I and II are known as the silent killer. If you don't control it then it will control you. Knowing me, I have always had to learn the hard way so let me share this lesson with you.

One should check one's blood sugar and check it often. Be sure to take your prescribed medicine or insulin shots as you are instructed to do by your doctor. By not doing so, you are not only jeopardizing your self but your fellow bikers as well.

It was a hot summer! Beautiful sparkling stars reflected off of a bright perfectly shaped full moon. Myself and other members of the "P's" Motorcycle Club were attending a field meet held by the "ROOTS" Motorcycle Club. It was a fun filled evening. I even won a first place trophy in the beer drinking contest. First time ever winning anything!

As we departed the event, I remember pulling out into the road but that is the last thing I remembered. We traveled several miles, which I don't remember but obviously we did, in fact, cover several miles because when I "woke up" I was sitting in the middle of Highway 288. My friends were asking me if I was alright and I felt a stiffness in my arms and legs. As they picked me up and carried me to the side of the road, I could see several bikes and cars pulling over and people running to my aid. I remember thinking to myself, "what the h--- just happened?"

When the ambulance arrived with in short minutes, with help, I stumbled to sit in it while they checked my condition. I was sore all over my body! My friends said that I rolled on the pavement at least five or six times. I felt a stiffness in both arms, both shoulders, both knees, and pain over and beside my right eye.

I refused the trip to the hospital because even though I was badly bruised and had a loss of skin all over my body, I was conscious and in my right frame of mind. I knew that if I went to the hospital they would find out that I had been drinking alcoholic beverages, thus a charge of DWI. So I chose to dodge that bullet!

I hadn't drank enough to be intoxicated because I know my limits. As I found out, drinking and diabetes just don't mix.

It was two days later before I realized that my blood sugars was totally out of control, also my road-rash was not healing properly. Reluctantly but mind soothing, I went to the emergency room and finally started on my road to recovery.

This is when I was told that I had suffered from a diabetic coma, due to not taking my meds for a few days along with drinking a small amount of alcohol. The coma happened while riding my "bike" and I don't remember when, where, or how it happened – but it happened. I wear the scars like medals to prove it! It's only by the blessings and the grace from GOD that I am here today to write about it. Thank you, Father GOD for wrapping your loving arms around me!

So, "Please! Please! Please!" if you are a diabetic, stay on top of it and keep it under control. The life you save may just be your own!

Jay "Spoons" Collins
Delbarton, WV

"Big Joe" of Houston, Texas RIP

BIKER UNITY (WRITTEN FOR THE FALL)

Well, my biker friends, the time has come where in some parts of the country we start putting our bikes "up" for the winter months. Some of us will be "tearing them down" for repainting or replacing parts, getting them ready for the next summer.

But then again, in other parts of the country, we are fortunate that the winter weather doesn't get all that bad and with the exception of a few weeks, we can still ride on a daily or weekly basis. At any rate, there is one form of "Biker Unity" that I think should prevail for all of us and it doesn't take but a quick second and very little effort, if any. It makes you feel good inside and gives you a feeling of respect while at the same time "giving" the feeling of respect. I'm sure some of you have already been doing this. In fact, I know that you have because you've done it to me.

The point I'm trying to make is: While you are riding down the road, cruising at 60 – 70 – or 100 (smiles) miles an hour and you see another biker or group of bikers coming the opposite direction, it doesn't hurt to lift your left hand in the air and give the speaking gesture or the "high five," thumbs-up, or peace sign like we did back in the 70's. Try it sometime!

You get the feeling of even though you may be out there alone, by choice or otherwise, you still have a friend, a form of bonding, if you will, even if it's only in passing and you are respected for being the type of person that you are, a lover of motorcycles and the love of being out there on the open road. Not only that, but can you imagine what the drivers of automobiles are thinking when they see bikers of all colors speaking to each other while riding down the road? Especially if they've been behind you for miles and miles or state to state. They probably think that we all know each other (SMILE). That's just our common bond showing! After all, we as bikers are a creed of our own and we have an understanding about life (and in one way or another), that only we share.

So throw your hands up in the air – wave them like you just don't care! Tell somebody – anybody! I'm a biker and don't care if you stare! (ha ha ha).

BIKER UNITY! GOTTA HAVE IT! GOTTA LOVE IT! RIDE HARD! RIDE SAFE!

Left to Right:
Henry "Boots Scooter" Moody; Raleigh "Tracker"
Jackson; Roy "Storm" Norman; Donald "DJ"
Jackson; Delaristo "Bus Coole" Stillgess

Tru Cons of Houston, Texas

I YEARN

I yearn to ride a "FAT BOY"
Though impossible it may seem
The "FAT BOY" is the big boy's toy
This is my life-long dream

I yearn to ride a "ROAD KING"
So badly – I'm going insane
I'm currently riding a "GOLD WING"
So I do not dare complain

I yearn to ride a "DYNA-GLIDE'
Yet, a "SPORTSTER' would get me loose
I'd ride them each with so much pride
And would love to ride a "DEUCE"

I yearn to ride a "SPRINGER"
A "HERITAGE SOFTTAIL" – for me
I'll tell you no lie ------ My "HONDA" is fly
But a "HARLEY" is my destiny!

George Webster

TJ Jones and his wife TamSue

CHROMED OUT
(The Beginning)

Once upon a time there were two men
With a lot in common it may seem
Even though they were "Johnsons" they were not kin
Yet, Boggs and L.B. had the same dream

They released their hidden inhibition
For they realized they had goals and ideals
So they set forth – on a mission
God had blessed them with talents and skills

"Tommie Runner" and her mother "Stanlee"
"Laid out" the graphic designs and such
And wives by their side and behind them
"Karen" and "Jan" with their magical touch

The best motorcycle magazine in Texas
Truly the best without a doubt,
Take it from me and you will agree
The cream of the crop is "Chromed Out"

Left to Right: Alex "Doc" Gross, Jr.; Roy "Storm"
Norman; Raleigh "Tracker" Jackson

Roy "Storm" Norman RIP

ROUGH
JUSTICE

CHAPTER ONE

It was 10 a.m., Monday morning on a beautiful spring day. Mary Jones was sitting in the outpatient lounge at the Grant Hospital Psychiatric Ward. Patiently waiting, she watched an old lady, about seventy-five in her years, slowly walk down the hall with one yellow sock on one foot and a red sock on the other. She had on one of those white gowns that is normally worn in a hospital – the type that has no back to it. As she walked, she would spray a can of fly spray towards her bare bottom. Suddenly, a nurse appears and says, "Now Miss Mildred, you know you're not supposed to be out here. Now you get back to your room, okay?"

As the friendly nurse helps Miss Mildred along, she smiles at Mary and says, "Your husband will be out in a few minutes." Mary smiled back at her and nodded her head. Mary was a thirty-year-old who looked twenty. Her hair was long, down to her waist, and was dark silky brown. She had a well shaped body, and was a nice, kind, generous lady who worked hard all of her life as an accountant for several different wealthy people.

Mary and Elmo met a few years ago and got married after dating for a few months. Mary knew that Elmo had a mental problem, but she loved him anyway. As time passed, Elmo's problems became worse, and resulted to physical violence toward Mary. Elmo would become emotionally upset over the slightest things. He would then sometimes beat his wife violently. Sometimes Elmo would seem to be very normal. But often he would go into his nasty attitude and would always take it out on Mary. He would visit the hospital twice a month and for six hours each visit. He would be examined both mentally and medically. Each visit, Mary would be there waiting for Elmo to complete his testing and counseling.

They would go home and try to live a normal life but as time went on, it became more difficult. Elmo would slip easier into his violent temper more often and Mary would always take the beating and run to the bedroom and cry.

As Mary gazed out the large picture window, the voice of her husband could be heard coming down the hallway. Elmo appeared laughing and joking with the nurse. "I'm ready to go home," he said, as he leaned over and kissed Mary on the cheek. Mary smiled and stood up. They held hands as they walked through the doors. Elmo had a gentle look on his face and seemed to be content with himself. He was a large man who stood 6'6" and was all muscle – about 290 pounds of muscle. He was naturally well built.

CHAPTER TWO

A few months went by and Elmo seemed to be cured of his mental stress. He was starting to do good as far as controlling his temper and refraining from acts of violence. Elmo was very intelligent. At times it would seem as though he didn't even have a problem. He seemed as normal as everyone else. But who is to say what is normal? Maybe we're all a little lacking in the mental department.

One day Elmo was out in the garage working on his motorcycle. He had an old Harley Davidson. He was completely rebuilding the engine and repainting the body. The old Harley bike was his pride and joy. He also had a 57 Chevy. The engine in the Chevy badly needed rebuilding and he also was repairing the body and planned to paint the car also. Elmo would work on the bike and car whenever he got a chance to do so. Spending most of his time in the garage was the highlight of Elmo's life.

Suddenly the roar of another Harley pulled up into the driveway. It was one of Elmo's biker friends. Jessie was his name. Jessie was a fairly built man with tattoos on both arms and one large one on his chest. "What's going on, Elmo," Jessie asked, as he walked toward the garage. Elmo laid down his tools and opened the small refrigerator to get his friend a cold beer. They talked as they drank. Mary was watching from the kitchen window. She didn't care much for Elmo's friends because they always seemed to get Elmo in trouble.

She could barely hear the conversation, but she knew one thing: Jessie was mad about something. His voice would become loud, then soft, then loud again. Elmo started walking toward the kitchen door. Mary started doing the dishes, making herself look busy as if she hadn't heard the yelling coming from the men outside in the garage. Elmo walked in and went straight to the closet where he had his sawed-off double-barreled shotgun. He picked it up, loaded it and turned to put on his black leather vest, which had the name "HELL RAISERS" on the back. The vest also had a picture of a fire with a knife, sword, and a gun around it. "Don't go Elmo, please don't go," Mary cried. Elmo slapped her in the face with such force that she fell to the floor. "Don't ever tell me what to do!" he yelled at her.

Elmo stood over the very frightened woman and she could tell that she had a look in his eyes that could kill. He stared at her for a full minute, then turned and walked out the door. He walked out behind the garage and then all you could hear was loud thunder as Elmo pulled from the back on a big, black, beautiful Harley. Jessie fired up his bike and they both drove off. The loud thundering noise from both bikers roared down the streets of the city.

They turned into a parking lot that was filled with bikers. Fifty to sixty bikers congregated and as Elmo parked his beautiful Harley, the bikers surrounded him. "What's the deal?" Elmo asked, speaking to anyone and no one in particular. No one answered him. He noticed there was a sad look on everyone's face and a few had been crying.

"What the hell is going on here?" Elmo yelled with a boatload of frustration in his voice.

A man called "Bull Dog" stepped up said, "Elmo, it's your little brother Judd. He's been shot!" The look on Elmo's face was a mixture of stark madness, grief, and for a minute he was in a state of shock. Sweat started pouring down his face. "Follow me," said Bull Dog, as he started walking to the clubhouse. Elmo followed and others followed him. He entered the clubhouse and there lying on the floor was Judd. He wasn't dead, but very close to it.

"Judd!" Elmo cried, "Who did this to you? Why?" Elmo bent down and held his little brother in his arms as Judd tried to speak.

"It was Red Beard," Judd said, in a low whisper. "Red Beard," he repeated, "from Dayton, Ohio.

"Elmo, I…I…" just then, Judd's eyes rolled back into his head and his body became limp and heavy at the same time. Elmo hugged his little brother and cried as the others walked out the door with sad hearts and angry faces.

"Who in the hell is Red Beard?" Elmo yelled. Jodi, a pretty blue-eyed blonde wearing a leather jacket and jeans, stepped up and said, "I know him. He is a hired hit man from Dayton," she said. She went on to say, "He has a gang of tough women bikers and they all have red hair. He has a bald head and wears a thick, red beard. I think they call themselves 'The Red Raiders.' or some shit like that." Then Elmo stared at the ground. Everyone knew what he was thinking. Revenge! Revenge! Revenge!

Elmo pulled himself together and told Jodi, a guy named Slick Rick, and about four others to pack up and go to Dayton. "Put a tail on this Red Beard bastard and don't make a move on him. After you find out where he lives and hangs out, two of you come back and let me know." They all jumped on their Harleys and rode off. In the meantime, Elmo said "Jessie," in a stern voice, "would you go ahead and make funeral arrangements and get back with me?"

"Sure, Elmo, sure," Jessie replied. Elmo fired up his big, black shiny Harley and rode off. The others stood around in small groups talking and gaining the inward feeling of "sweet revenge."

CHAPTER THREE

Mary was putting dinner on the table when Elmo walked in. He immediately hugged his wife and broke into tears. "What's wrong?" she asked. Elmo cried loudly now, as they held each other tighter. "It's Judd," Elmo said, as he brought himself back together. "My little brother is dead." "Oh my God," Mary said. They both embraced each other for what seemed like an hour, but it was really only a few minutes. Elmo and Mary sat down to the dinner table, but neither could eat. They just sat there, both in a sullen stare.

Elmo finally left the table and went to the bedroom and laid across the bed. He sobbed like a little kid. He had flashbacks in his mind of when he and Judd used to play together as children. From tossing a football back and forth to working on car engines until the wee hours of the night. He remembered how Judd used to be so happy to get his first mini-bike, then his first car. Thoughts flashed in Elmo's mind as he fell fast asleep. Mary peeked in on him and decided to let him sleep. A few hours later, Mary sat beside him and slowly started rubbing his back. Elmo awakened and rolled over, pulled Mary down to him and kissed her with much passion.

She returned his kisses with an abundance of passion coming from her heart through her lips. Elmo responded by slowly undressing her and at the same time she was undressing him. He started sucking her tits while at the same time, she caressed his dick and balls. He stuck his dick inside her hot walls of love and they fucked madly for several minutes. They both moaned and groaned and the closer they reached an orgasm, the louder they moaned and groaned. Suddenly, Mary started screaming and Elmo was yelling, "Yes! Yes! Yes!" They both reached climax at the same time. Their bodies were drenched with sweat. They held each other close and lightly kissed as the tenderness of their kisses brought Elmo's staff to attention again. He fucked his wife for several minutes more and exploded his warm juice inside her hot pussy again. They laid together and softly fell to sleep.

CHAPTER FOUR

The next few days went by fast. Elmo spent all of his time pumping iron, getting his body ready for the task of destroying Red Beard. The day of the funeral finally came. Bikers came from all around. Some even came from far away states. Several different clubs and gangs came to pay their respect to the young dead man called Judd. Black bikers, White bikers, as well as Hispanic bikers. They were all there. Over one thousand bikers in all showed up. Some of the bikers didn't even know Judd, but due to the fact that he was a biker, that's all they needed to know. That's how the bikers were though. It's like an unwritten law. If you're a biker, then you've got to be all right. Some people don't understand it, but it's like a "biker's creed."

The funeral lasted about a half of an hour. They lowered Judd's casket into the grave and then lowered his bike down on top of his casket. Elmo picked up the shovel and tossed in the first scoop of dirt. He handed the shovel to his wife, Mary. And she tossed in the second scoop of dirt. Others fell in line and followed until the grave was fully covered. Suddenly, Elmo pulled out his nine-millimeter pistol and fired a shot in the air; then the whole crowd of bikers, over one-thousand of them, pulled out guns and they all shot a round into the air. The atmosphere was full of loud thunder as their shots echoed through the cemetery. The smell of gunpowder was thick in the air.

Elmo pulled out a small pint of whiskey, took a big sip, then poured the rest on Judd's grave. Several others followed suite. Toasting their last toast with the young dead man, who now lay in his grave. Everyone jumped on their bikes and the roar of engines filled the air. From miles away you could hear the rolling thunder of over one-thousand motorcycles. The sound was frightening and yet exciting to the ears of people who were not bikers. It was a beautiful sight to see – so many motorcycles in one place at the same time. Different colors, different makes and models, and different races of men riding them. A beautiful, beautiful sight!

As they departed, some clubs left the city and rode back to their prospective cities and states. Others went to the "Hell Raisers Clubhouse" to have a few beers. Most of them went on to their own clubhouses spread across the city.

CHAPTER FIVE

Elmo, Mary and their closer friends went to Elmo's house and sort of kicked back and relaxed. Jessie stayed a little while and went back to the clubhouse. Bull Dog and his best friend, Wild Man from Cambridge, Ohio, drank a few more beers and they too left so that Elmo and Mary could be alone.

Elmo sat in the big over-stuffed chair, his favorite, and thought of the beautiful funeral that he had just given his little brother. Since his parents were both killed in an automobile accident three years ago, he had no one left but his devoted wife, Mary. So, Elmo decided he wanted a son to carry on his family name. "Mary, honey," he called, "would you like to have a son?" Mary came out of the kitchen and smiled as she walked right past the large over-stuffed chair Elmo was sitting in. Walking straight towards the bedroom, while shedding her clothes, Elmo finally got the hint as to what her answer was. Elmo jumped up, pulled his pants down and followed Mary to the bedroom. They made love with great passion. They then showered, went to the kitchen, ate a ham sandwich and fifteen minutes later was back in the bedroom – fucking again like it was going out of style. This time they went to sleep, exhausted from a long day.

CHAPTER SIX

Several weeks passed and Elmo started to become worried about the whereabouts of Jodi and Slick Rick and their four companions. While Elmo was working, Jodi and Slick Rick infiltrated Red Beard's clubhouse posing as a couple of lost souls from New York City. They became quite friendly with Red Beard and his all-female, red-headed gang. Slick Rick started an affair with Sadie Matthews, a pretty, sexy red-head who always wore leather clothing. They had become quite a hot ticket. Jodi was busy keeping Red Beard occupied. Most of the other female members were all bull dykes. They loved to make love to each other, although each and every one of them would take their turn going to bed with their fearless leader, Red Beard. After a few days went by, the other four members of Elmo's club were picked up by the police for "suspicious characters." While locked up in the county jail, they had gotten into a fight with a local gang of hoods. Someone was killed and all four men were charged with murder.

In the meantime, Jodi and Slick Rick could not get away to notify Elmo for fear it would blow their cover. So they decided to wait until the time was right to get away. As time passed, Slick Rick would go to the other biker clubs such as "Bad to the Bone" and "The Harley Boyz," both Black clubs and both on West Third Street. He would pick up bits and pieces from the Black brothers as to how to catch Red Beard at his weakest times. He also hung out at "The Toros" and "The Road Runners" clubhouses.

At the time, Wild Dog was president of the "Road Runners," Dayton Chapter. Slick Rick became friendly with Wild Dog and Big Frank. He thought this friendship with the Brothers might pay off someday; little did he know he was so right. While at the Road Runners clubhouse on South Euclid Street, Slick Rick called Elmo long distance and told him what was going on. Elmo was glad to hear him. He told Slick Rick to "hang in there" and he instructed him to contact him at least once a week to keep him informed on the activities of Red Beard.

"You and Jodi are doing a great job, my brother," said Elmo. "I am very proud of you, and please let Jodi know that when it all comes down, I'll owe both of you a big one," Elmo said as Slick Rick said, "It's a pleasure to help a good brother like you."

They said their good-byes and hung up. Slick Rick handed a five dollar bill to Wild Dog and said, "Thanks for the use of the phone, my brother." Wild Dog took the five dollar bill and immediately gave it to Running Man, who was working the bar, and told him to bring himself and Slick Rick a couple of shots of whiskey. The men smiled and drank together. "What are friends for," said Wild Dog, "if they can't help each other now and then."

Just then, the sound of two bikes pulled up in front of the clubhouse. It was Tru Harris, the President of the Springfield Chapter of the Road Runners and Bob "The Kid" McConnell, who was the Vice President, and Bus Coole, the founder of the Springfield Roadrunners. Big Frank and Blue greeted Tru, Bus Coole and the Kid out on the front porch. After a few high-fives and small talk, they all entered the clubhouse and Bus Coole bought a round of beer for everybody. Slick Rick took a likening to Bus right off the bat. Bus called him his blue-eyed Soul Brother. Slick Rick liked that. They acted as if they had always known each other, even though they had just met for the first time less than an hour ago. This is the effect Bus had on a lot of people. Maybe that's why they called him Bus Coole.

As Coole and Slick Rick became closer friends, they found out that they had a lot in common. They both had the same kind of bikes, they both drank Tanguray, and they both were smooth talkers and had tempers that would flare up at the drop of a hat.

CHAPTER SEVEN

Meanwhile, back in Columbus, some sixty-five miles away. Elmo was still pumping iron and getting bigger and stronger. He knew the day would come when he would have to call on all of the strength his body could muster. Because he wanted to kill Red Beard with his bare hands.

As Elmo finished his weight lifting for the day, the phone rang. "Hello," he said. "Hello, honey" as Mary's voice came through the line. "I just called to tell you that I'm on my way home and I've got good news for you." Elmo could envision the smile on her face as she talked. "OK," Elmo answered, "I'll be waiting for you." They hung up and Elmo went to the kitchen and pulled frozen steaks out of the freezer. This will do just fine for dinner, he thought to himself.

He walked out into the garage and began to work on the 57 Chevy. He fixed up a board of putty and started filling in the dents and small holes. He turned on his radio and one of his favorite songs was playing. It was "The Wall" by Pink Floyd. "We don't need no education," the song played as Elmo sang along with it.

Some of the words he didn't know, so he hummed along until he got to the part where it said, "Hey! Teachers! Leave those kids alone!" Elmo sang that part out loudly. It brought memories to his mind of his little brother, Judd. He remembered when he and Judd used to ride their bicycles to school and lock them up together with combination locks so that no one would steal them. He remembered one day someone tried to steal them and because they were locked, the thief became frustrated and bent all of the spokes with the pounding of a brick. Elmo remembered the look on his little brother's face when he first laid eyes on his broken wheels and spokes. A sad, forlorn look of a boy that couldn't believe that his new bicycle was now all messed up.

Elmo remembered how he found out who had done it and how he and Judd kicked their asses. Elmo then had the vision in his mind of how it was the first time Judd had ever hit anyone. It was Judd's first fight. He was only six years old. He was scared at first, mainly because the boy who crushed his bike was ten years old and somewhat bigger than Judd. "Fight him!" Elmo hollered. As Elmo started hitting the other ten year old, who was his own size and age, Judd started fighting with the other boy. All of the kids on the playground stopped playing and gathered around to watch the fight. Elmo remembered how he fought hard and finally beat up the kid. The kid took off running as Elmo gave chase. Elmo tackled him and hit him twice in the face until blood ran down his nose.

At that moment he heard young Judd screaming for help. Elmo ran over to pull the bigger kid off of Judd and hit him in the stomach. The kid lost his breath for a few seconds. When he regained his breath, he suddenly took off running. Elmo hugged his little brother in victory as the other kids patted them both on their backs. The other kids found relief and satisfaction in seeing the two bullies get beat up. Elmo and Judd felt a large sense of pride and since that day, they always fought together. They gained the respect of all the other kids throughout their early years in school.

As Elmo sat there, lost in the past, Mary drove up into the driveway. She got out of the car and was smiling from ear to ear. They kissed and Elmo followed her into the house. "Why are you happy?" Elmo asked. "Oh, you'll see," she answered as she began preparing dinner. "I see you put out steaks," she said. "Yeah, I have a taste for it today. I hope you don't mind," he said. "Of course not," she replied. "Whatever you want is fine with me." Elmo gave Mary a kiss on her lips, then he strolled into the living room. He sat in his favorite chair and picked up the remote control, turning on the tv. The news was on. He watched it dramatically as firemen were fighting a huge fire across town. He felt sorry for the seven children who were found dead from smoke inhalation. He felt like going to help fight the fire, but he thought he'd better leave that to the firemen.

Mary came in and sat on his lap and they kissed and giggled as he tickled her ear with his tongue. Elmo and Mary were very much in love and they were all each other had in life. So Elmo thought! "Honey," Mary said. "The reason I took so long to come home today was because I had been sitting in the doctor's office for the last three hours." A serious look came on Elmo's face. "What's wrong," he asked, "Are you alright?"

"Sure. I'm fine," she said, smiling, "and so is the baby."

At first Elmo looked dumb-founded. Then he screamed with joy and said, "You mean...you mean... are you telling me that...that we're going to have a..a..a... baby?" Elmo could hardly get it out he was so excited. "Yes," Mary answered. Elmo kissed her and then jumped up running through the house yelling, "Yes! Yes! Alright! This calls for a beer," he said. He opened the refrigerator and got a beer and a glass of milk. He knew Mary didn't like beer, so he poured the milk for her and they toasted.

Even though Elmo was happy, as he thought to himself he was torn between happiness and sadness. Happy because he really wanted a child, hopefully a boy, and sad because he thought of how sad it would be if he didn't survive the attack on Red Beard. He was starting to have mixed emotions now. But he didn't want to think about it. For the moment all he wanted was to enjoy the thought of having a son to carry on his name.

The phone rang. "Hello," answered Elmo. "Hello, Mr. Jones?" the voice asked. "Yes, this is he," answered Elmo. "How may I help you?" "This is Bob Finch from down the street. I was wondering if you could find the time, would you fix my car for me?" "What's the problem," Elmo asked. "Well, it did have a loud ticking noise coming from the engine, but now it won't even start." "Sounds like your engine might have blown," replied Elmo. "What's your address," Elmo asked. "I'll come take a look at it." "Forty-seven Walnut," the voice answered, "just right down the street." "I'll be there within the hour," Elmo said. They hung up the phone and Elmo went back to his favorite chair. "I'm going to go down the street and check on Bob Finch's car. I think it may need the motor rebuilt," he said to Mary, as she looked at him with a curious expression on her face. She knew that Elmo was good at working on engines and so did the people in his neighborhood. This is how Elmo made his living. He would work on cars for people. He could fix anything from bumper to bumper. He had planned to open his own garage and go into the legit business of automobile mechanics, but he just never got around to it. He would have had a business if he would set his mind to it, but as long as people like Bob Finch were around and needed his talent or skills to fix their cars, he could still make money without all the overhead,

About twenty minutes had passed and Elmo decided to go check out the ailing automobile. When he arrived, a large German Sheperd greeted him with loud barking and snarling teeth. Elmo decided to wait in the car until Bob came out of the house. Bob came out and took "Nero" to the back yard and put him in the kennel. Elmo could tell that Bob took good care of the large dog because his kennel was about eight feet tall and fifty feet long and six feet wide. It was very clean inside with a modern built dog house, complete with carpet inside and shingle roofing. Elmo admired a man who took care of his dog. As Bob was putting Nero away, Elmo had a sudden flashback of how Judd loved his dog, "Chief." He envisioned in his mind how Judd used to throw a ball for Chief to fetch and while Chief was fetching, Judd would go and hide. Judd would laugh long and loud when Chief would finally find him and start licking his face.

"I'm glad you stopped by," Bob said, as the vision of Judd vanished from Elmo's head. "I'm glad you caught me at a good time," Elmo replied. "Let's take a look at the patient and see what the Doc can do for her," Elmo said playfully. Bob's car was a classic 1926 Model T Ford. It was in immaculate condition and, as well as expected, seeing that Bob was an expert auto detailer. Of course, he kept that old black Model T shiny as black ice.

They checked the car out and immediately Elmo knew the problem. It was as he already expected. The motor needed rebuilding. They came to an agreement and Elmo would repair the motor. He tied a burlap rope on the bumpers and while Elmo drove, Bob steered his car and they pulled it down to Elmo's house. They pulled it into the back yard and then Elmo took Bob back home. Before Elmo returned home, he stopped at the fish market on East Broad Street and picked up some cod. He ran into an old friend in the store and talked for a few minutes. "I'll be damned," Elmo said as he laid eyes on Jason.

Jason was a thin built, but muscular Black man. They had known each other for quite awhile. They shook hands. "I'm sorry to hear about your little brother," Jason said apologetically. "Did you ever find out who did it," Jason asked. "Yes, I found out and believe me, my friend, his days are numbered. It was a guy they call Red Beard out of Dayton," Elmo said. "I know that motherfucker," Jason replied. "He's got a bald head and runs with a lot of red head bitches," he asked. "Yeah, that's him," Elmo said disgustingly. "Watch him," said Jason, "He's a dangerous one. Don't turn your back on him because he's a dirty son of a bitch." Jason was also a good friend of Bus Coole's. They used to run together, fight together, and chase women together. That is, if the women weren't chasing them. Elmo and Jason shook hands again and parted company.

Elmo was on his way back home now. As he pulled into the driveway, he couldn't help but think about the good times when Judd used to want to go skating to an all Black roller rink just to watch Trigger skate. He loved to watch him stride across the floor, ducking and dodging hundreds of other skaters, without missing a beat. Yeah, Elmo thought to himself, those were the gold ole days. Just then Mary stuck her head out of the door and yelled to Elmo, "Are you going to sit in the car all day or are you coming in?" Elmo snapped out of his daze and walked into the house. "How did you know I wanted cod," she asked as she opened the package. "I've been craving it all day," she said. "I don't know," answered Elmo. "I've been kind of craving it too."

As Mary started to cook the cod fish, Elmo decided to step into the shower. By the time he came out of the shower, the fish was cooked and ready to eat. Elmo and Mary sat down and broke bread.

After they finished eating, Elmo went out and started tearing down the motor in his neighbor's car. He worked on it until dark. He decided to call it a day and put away his tools, making a mental note of the parts that he needed to repair the motor.

The next day, Elmo and Mary ate bacon, eggs, and grits for breakfast. Today was the day that Elmo had to go to the hospital for his mental stress treatment. They decided to call Mary's doctor to find out if it would be alright to visit him for her check-up, since she would already be at the hospital anyway. The doctor said yes, so they would be able to "kill two birds with one stone." When they arrived at the hospital, they were a little early so they stopped in the cafeteria and had coffee. As they drank their coffee, they noticed a young couple that had just signed out to take their new baby home. They couldn't help but notice how happy the couple seemed.

While the couple walked out of the cafeteria, Elmo and Mary held hands and kissed, just like the younger couple had done. An older nurse in her late 50's walked up to them and said, "Mrs. Jones, the doctor is ready to see you now." Mary kissed Elmo as she walked away with the nurse. "I'll meet you back here when I'm through, honey," Elmo said, "because I won't have to stay the whole six hours today." Mary nodded her head as they waved good-bye. About fifteen minutes passed and another nurse came to get Elmo. "Are you ready, Mr. Jones?" she asked. "I guess so," Elmo replied hesitantly. He really didn't want to go and the nurse could hear it in his voice. Mary came back to the cafeteria and bought a piece of cherry pie and a piece of apple pie. She also bought a piece of cake for Elmo. She waited about forty-five minutes and Elmo finally appeared. He was smiling as he sat down.

"Why are you smiling like a Chessy cat," she asked. "I don't know," was his reply. "Why are you eating a cherry and an apple pie?" Elmo asked. "Well," she said, "I bought the cake for you," as she slid it over to him, "and I bought the cherry pie for one of them and the apple pie for the other," she smiled. "They are getting hungry," she said. "Do you mean to tell me that…that.. we are going to have tw…tw…tw…?" Elmo couldn't get it out.

"Yes." Mary answered with a bright smile that lit up the whole room. "Yes, we're going to have twins." "Two…two..two of them?" he asked in astonishment. "Yes, two of them," she answered. Suddenly Mary yelled, "Nurse! Nurse! Please help me!" At that second, three nurses came running over to help revive Elmo, for he had passed out, right there on the spot! The nurses and even Mary couldn't help but laugh.

Elmo awakened as they held smelling salt under his nose. "Whew!" Elmo said, sounding relieved. "I thought for a minute there you said that we were having twins."

"I did." Mary said. The nurses caught him again.

CHAPTER EIGHT

Meanwhile, sixty-five miles away, Jodi and Slick Rick were still on the fast track. Slick Rick managed to con two older women into falling in love with him. He had no intentions of loving either one of them. All he wanted was their fat bank accounts. He wined and dined both of them and swindled them out of large sums of money. Neither of the ladies knew about the other. No wonder they called him "Slick Rick." He definitely had his way with women. The money that he had taken from them wasn't for himself. He hired the best lawyer in Dayton to represent his four companions who were charged with murder. Mr. Fischer was determined to at least get the charges reduced.

As it happened, three of the men were set free on a five thousand dollar bond and the fourth man escaped. Slick Rick paid the Bail Bondsman and the lawyer under a false name. He then gave the men $1,000 each and told them to "get lost." Needless to say, the Four comrades were gone in a hurry. Where – no one knows, but they didn't go back to Columbus. Slick Rick had a feeling that they might have gone separate ways. In the meantime, Slick Rick continued to play on the rich elderly ladies and lived rather well.

Jodi also was living well. By now, Red Beard was madly in love with the beautiful blonde. He tried desperately to make her dye her hair red, but she wasn't having it. This is one of the reasons why he loved her because he couldn't control her. Little did he know that she was on a mission. She really didn't like to go to bed with him but she knew she had to in order to keep an eye on him, and his habits. Every time she thought of her young friend Judd, lying in his grave, she could become full of hatred toward the big bald-headed bastard. But she did a good job of concealing her true feelings. She even knew enough now to put Red Beard away behind bars for the rest of his life. She had witnessed some of the things that he had done.

One day Red Beard and his gang hid their bikes in an old run down warehouse. They had broken the lock and set up camp right there in the warehouse, as if they owned it. Red Beard sent out a scout to keep an eye on a rival gang called "The Blue Devils." It was a small gang of about ten members. Red Beard's gang had a total of thirty-one members. The Blue Devils could hold their own. Most other gangs in the city wouldn't fuck with them. They were a treacherous bunch. More of a crazy breed than anything else.

Red Beard's gang didn't have any certain grudge against them, they just didn't like the idea of the Blue Devils moving into their side of the city. Red's gang stayed in the vacant warehouse for more than five hours.

Waiting patiently as they snorted and shot up Crack. They wore their weapons openly and bold. Knives and guns were common to be seen on the muscular-built, red haired bitches. Finally, the scout that Red sent out came back and told of how the other gang's clubhouse was now empty. They had all just left it. Red Beard and his gang left their bikes and walked the half block around the corner to the home of the Blue Devils. They busted down the back door and went inside.

They tore the place up.

They started by cutting up the two pool tables with their long 12" knives. They broke every mirror and glass in the place. They drank the liquor and beer as they trashed the place. What they didn't drink, they stacked into boxes and set them beside the door to take with them. Someone smashed the jukebox and took the money out of it. They raided the ice box and took all of the food. Red Beard told four of the bitches to take the food and liquor to the warehouse and to hurry back. As they obeyed his command, Red Beard pulled out his big red hairy dick and pissed all over the floor. He held his head back and let out a spine-curling howl. Just like a rabid wolf. They continued to trash the place until the four bitches came back from hauling out the goods.

Suddenly the sound of roaring motorcycles could be heard a block away. The Blue Devils were coming back. Red Beard had a sudden look of panic on his face, then he ordered everyone to hide. They all hid behind the bar and turned over booths and tables. Several hid in the bathrooms. They could now hear the motorcycles approaching and as the engines were silent, the Blue Devils had no ideas of what laid waiting for them. The Blue Devils walked in with anger building up in their hearts. They stood there, speechless. The club was in total silence. Then suddenly Red Beard jumped up from behind the bar and stood on top of it. He opened his mouth with a loud war cry and beat his chest just like a wild ape.

The red headed bitches came out of hiding and surrounded the ten Blue Devils. Red Beard pointed at the leader of the other gang and growled like a wild bear. The leader of the Blue Devils growled back and Red Beard dived toward him and the fight was on. The whole room exploded into violence as the bitches plowed into the ten Blue Devils. Chairs and bottles were flying in the air. The hard-core bitches were fighting with the Blue Devil men as if they were men themselves. At first it was fists and feet only. Then the stone cold shiny steel blades were drawn and then blood was splashing everywhere.

The Blue Devils were fighting with fearless eyes. You could tell that they knew how to fight. But the odds were against them. They were outnumbered three to one. The Blue Devils were being destroyed as they tried desperately to defend their clubhouse. The last two Blue Devils were still fighting. The leader and his right-hand man. Suddenly a knife from out of the air found its mark right in the center of his back. The right-hand man fell forward, face first, hitting the floor with a heavy thud. The leader was the only one left. He stood in the middle of the floor, surrounded by red hair bitches. Red Beard jumped up on the top of the bar again. He looked at the leader of the Blue Devils and yelled, "On your knees, you Son of a bitch! Bow down to me and beg for mercy and I'll let you live," Red Beard roared.

The fearless leader looked around him. He saw his gang lying on the floor with their throats cut and knives sticking out of them. They all laid in puddles of blood. He then looked at each one of the bitches. One by one, he stared in their faces. Then he looked up at Red Beard, his breathing becoming heavier. Suddenly he yelled at the top of his voice, "Fuck You! I bow to no one!" At that instant, Red Beard pulled out a large dagger and threw it at the leader and it landed right in the middle of his forehead. The fearless leader stood for a few seconds and then fell straight back as if he were a tree that had just been chopped down.

Red Beard jumped down from the bar, walked over to him and pulled the dagger out of his head, wiped the blood on his chest and spit on him. Then Red Beard let out a loud laugh and the bitches laughed as they left the shambled clubhouse. When they got halfway back to the warehouse, Red Beard noticed that Jodi wasn't there with them. He became worried that she had been hurt or even killed, so he turned and ran full speed back to the Blue Devil's clubhouse. He ran inside and called Jodi's name. He heard sobbing, crying coming from the corner and as he walked toward the muffled cry, he could see where a large man, a member of the Blue Devils, was stretched across the floor with a knife in his back, pinning Jodi on the floor. His two hundred seventy-five pound frame covered her one hundred twenty pound body and she was trapped.

Red Beard removed the large man by turning him over and then he helped Jodi to her feet. She cried loudly then and wrapped her arms around the big man called Red Beard. Just then, two of Red Beard's gang members came in and poured gasoline all over everything. As they all left, they poured a stream of gasoline all the way as they walked. When they got to the corner, they turned, being on the other side of a corner building. Red Beard lit a match, fired up a cigarette and dropped the match on the stream of gasoline. Seconds later there was a very loud explosion and the whole clubhouse went up in flames.

Red Beard and his gang stayed in the abandoned warehouse and drank the beer and liquor that they had stolen from the now dead and defunct Blue Devils. They partied as the sounds of fire truck sirens passed the warehouse, headed for the tremendous fire. They all partied except Jodi. She was in a state of shock, for she had never seen anything like this before. She thought to herself that these people are really crazy and she had to find a way to warn Elmo. As she pulled herself together, she was privately working out a plan in her own mind.

CHAPTER NINE

On the other side of town, Slick Rick was still operating on a smooth level. He would be less suspicious of any wrong doing by not hanging too close to Red Beard's gang. Jodi would contact him by phone every few days to keep him informed of her whereabouts. The phone rang. "Hello," said Slick Rick. "This is Jodi," the voice on the other end said as it sounded cool and calm. "I need to meet you this Sunday at two p.m. at Donato's Pizza on West Sullivant Street," she said. "Don't forget. Two p.m." The phone went dead in his ear as she hung up.

Rick sat in the living room in his black velvet robe. He sipped on a freshly mixed rum and coke as he wondered what Jodi was going to talk to him about. Gina stood in the bedroom doorway. She was the rich real estate lady who had fallen in love with Slick Rick. She knew him only as Rick and that's how he wanted it. She was barefoot and dressed only in a man's white tee shirt. It was Rick's tee shirt and it was very large on her, but Gina in an oversized tee shirt looked about twenty times sexier than most women would have looked in sexy silk lingerie.

She stood, leaning against the door frame, her short blonde hair hanging down over her eyes, her beautiful legs crossed and her arms folded across her protruding tits. The sight of her would make any man sexually aroused. But Slick Rick wasn't just any man. He refused to be putty in any woman's hands. She had to work hard to gain his attention and affections. He picked up the newspaper and began to read it, paying less attention to the older love goddess. She felt offended. "Why don't you love me?" she asked. Slick Rick laid the paper down and looked at her as he motioned for her to come and sit beside him. She did. He held her hand and said, "Gina, I like you a hell of a lot. I really do, but I don't love you. I was hurt once from a love affair and I vowed never to love again. You understand, don't you?" he asked. "I'm not sure if I'm even capable of loving again," he said sadly.

From the look in Gina's eyes, he could tell that she was falling for his bullshit. So he laid it on thicker. "I want to love you but I just can't right now," he said. "Once I get my finances together like I want it, then I can start relaxing and concentrate more on being in a good love relationship. Please try to understand," he said. "I do understand, Rick, honey," she said. She leaned to him and they kissed. She opened his robe and started kissing his hairy chest. Slick Rick knew what was coming next because he knew that Gina loved to give him head. Just as he thought, she started sucking his pecker. She sucked and licked slowly at first and then faster and faster. He felt the volcano eruption starting in the bottom of his hard staff as it grew and grew until it exploded hot juice into her mouth. She moaned as she hummed the Campbell's soup commercial. "Um um good!" She licked his dick like it was a lollipop so as not to miss any of the warm juice.

Slick Rick laid back on the couch and she laid her head on his stomach. They lay there – both satisfied. He because he loved getting his dick sucked and she because she loved sucking dick. They laid there speechless. Deep into their own thoughts. It seemed like hours. Gina thought to herself that she would do anything to make Rick happy, so she suddenly jumped up and went to the bedroom. When she came back, she had two thousand dollars in one hundred dollar bills. "Here, honey," she said, as she laid it on his chest. "This will help you a little, I hope." Slick Rick acted as if he was in shock, but actually he had planned it this way. He played the game and he played it well. She was falling for him hook, line, and sinker.

Slick Rick kissed her and gently laid her on the plush carpet and plunged his meat deep into her juicy pussy. They rocked and rolled until they both reached an orgasm. Then they both rolled over and took a nap. A few hours passed. Slick Rick woke up and just laid there. He stared at Gina, thinking that she would be easy to fall in love with if he'd let himself do it. Thoughts of Faye entered his head while he still had Gina's dried cum on his dick. "I'll go to see Faye later today and spend some time with her," he thought to himself. He laid there another thirty minutes, wide awake. Finally, Gina woke up and said, "Rick, I think I love you." "Don't say that," Rick said, with expression in his voice. "Slow down. You're moving too fast." Just then, Slick Rick got up and went to take a shower. When he got back to the living room, he was fully dressed. "I'm going for a drive," he said as he walked toward the door. "I'll call you later," he said over his shoulder. Gina laid on the couch and began crying.

Slick Rick drove across town and just off of Morse Road, he pulled into a large driveway that led to a large, beautiful brick home. As he walked to the front door, Faye, the other woman he spent time with, met him at the door with arms opened wide. They kissed and hugged. "It's about time," she said. Faye was a short legged, big breasted woman. She was a cutie pie. She looked as if she was nineteen or twenty years old, but actually was fifty-three. She was firmly built with not an ounce of fat on her. Faye also had plenty of cash. Slick Rick made himself at home. He fixed them both a drink – a Scotch and water for her and a Tanguray on ice for himself. They cuddled on two large, round pillows on the floor and kissed several times.

"I need to talk to you about something very serious," Slick Rick said. She stopped smiling and began to look worried. "No, don't be alarmed," he said. "It's nothing bad." The look on her face started to relax now. He went on. "I'm transacting a deal to make a large sum of money, a very large sum," he said. "But I need more money to invest in order to make it work." "Sure," Faye said. "All you're after is my money." Seeing that there was a change that Faye might be on to him, he threw his acting skills into action.

"Fuck your money," he yelled. "I've got money of my own," as he reached into his pocket and brought out the two thousand dollars that Gina had just given him. "I'm not asking or begging you for your money," he said angrily. "I just thought that you might just want to help me. You can stick your money up your pretty ass!" Faye could see that she hurt his feelings, so she apologized. "I'm sorry," she said. "I just thought that you were after my money like everyone else is." "Well, I'm not everyone else," Slick Rick said, "and don't you ever forget it." Then Slick Rick thought he'd gamble a little and start walking out the door. "Wait! Wait!," Faye called. "Please don't go," she said. Slick Rick started inwardly smiling because she fell for the "silly mad game" that he was playing. He held in his smile so she wouldn't see it as he walked over to her and took her in his arms. As they hugged, he thought to himself, "This stupid bitch." Then he smiled.

They went to the bedroom and Slick Rick undressed her slowly as they kissed. Soon she was butt naked. He glowed at the beauty of her soft creamy white skin. He was still fully dressed as his meat became rock hard. She felt his meat and closed her eyes as if she were stepping into fantasy land. But this was real, she thought to herself. As he took off his own shirt and shoes, she unbuckled his belt buckle, unzipped his zipper, and pulled his pants down. As she pulled them down, his dick stood straight out and she dropped to her knees and took it into her mouth. Just as he started to bust a nut, she pulled it out and rubbed his dick all over her face. He shot a wad on her face and she moaned with her eyes closed.

He picked her up and sat her on the bed. She laid back and opened her legs wide. He dropped to his knees and began to suck her cunt. He sucked it for about ten minutes before she started screaming in ecstasy. Then he slid his dick into her and they fucked wildly until they both exploded together. They went to the shower and washed their bodies. Afterwards, they relaxed in front of the television and they both felt content with each other. Neither spoke. Slick Rick rubbed Faye's back as she drifted off into dreamland. He watched an old Bogart movie and finally joined her in deep sleep. The next morning when Slick Rick awakened, there was a check for two thousand dollars laying beside him and a note. The note read, "You were sleeping so good I didn't want to wake you. Take this to my bank and good luck with your investment venture. Love ya, Faye." Slick Rick hurried to the bank and cashed the check before she had a chance to change her mind. He smiled, all the way to the bank.

CHAPTER TEN

As time passed, Mary and Elmo were expecting the new additions to the family to arrive any day now. Mary was visiting the doctor's office more frequently. Everything seemed to be going alright. The unborn twins were healthy and so was the patiently waiting mother to be.

Elmo had been swamped with mechanical work from several people in the neighborhood as well as people from across town. Now that Mary wasn't able to work, Elmo doubled-up on his customers. He worked hard. Sometimes he would work on an engine all night. Or he would paint a car. At any rate, Elmo knew his way around an automobile's engine and he was one of the best body and paint men in the whole city of Columbus.

It was the first week in December. Snow had already fallen twice but there was no heavy accumulation. The wind was bitter cold that made the chill factor of about fifteen below zero.

Elmo and Mary decided to go up into the attic and sort through some old boxes and cabinets that Elmo's parents left. The attic was a dark, dingy small room. It was cluttered with all sizes of boxes and old trunks. Spider webs hung from the low beams and rafters. Small mouse holes could be seen along the dirty, dusty floor boards, along the walls. The room gave you the feeling of an old forgotten cave straight out of the twilight zone. As Elmo turned on the light, the sounds of tiny feet could be heard, scampering behind the mounds of cardboard boxes. "Let's not stay up here too long," Mary said. "We won't, you big chicken," was Elmo's reply as he playfully kissed his pregnant wife. They sorted through several boxes of old treasures. "Look at this," Elmo said, amazingly. He then pulled a stack of old newspapers out of a box. They were turning light brown in color but the print was still in very good condition.

The first newspaper that Elmo read was dated March 18, 1925. The headlines read, "Large Scale Tornado Disaster" Elmo read on, "689 people died, 13,000 injured, and $16 million to $18 million worth of damage occurred in 3 hours in the states of Indiana, Illinois, Kentucky, and Tennessee." He picked up another newspaper that read, "New Orleans, La. Opens the First College for Blacks, Xavier University, dated September 13, 1925." Elmo was becoming more excited as he picked up more old newspapers. "Look babe," Elmo said, "check this one out!" Elmo read on, "July 9, 1922, Johnny Weismuller from Alameda, California was the first swimmer to cover a distance of 100 meters, free-style, in less than one minute."

"I remember that guy," Elmo said, "he's the guy that played the first Tarzan character. Remember him?"

Elmo asked. "Yes, I remember the movies honey, but can we get out of here," Mary asked, "this place gives me the creeps." "Okay, I'm ready," Elmo replied. He dropped the old, torn at the edges newspapers, and they left the attic.

While Mary was taking a shower, Elmo sat in his favorite chair. While thinking about the old newspapers that he had just found, it reminded him of when he and Judd were young boys. He laid his head back in the comfortable chair and closed his eyes to better envision his memory. He remembered the day when their father took them to Wendover, Utah to see a man named Wilhelm Herz break a record. He remembered how his Dad was a motorcycle buff and how excited his Dad would get when it came to talking about fast motorcycles. This was back in 1956. August 4th, to be exact because he remembered that August 4 was the day that his Dad was born. That was his birthday present from Elmo's Mom, to go to Utah. Wilhelm Herz rode his motorcycle a measured mile over the salt flats at the speed of 210 m.p.h. Elmo remembered how they ate ice cream and cake in the back seat of the car. Judd was very young then and spilled ice cream all over everything.

Elmo smiled a peaceful smile as the thoughts vanished from his mind. Mary walked into the room and sat down on the couch. "Why are you smiling so much," she asked. "Oh, nothing," he answered. At that minute, Elmo dropped to his knees and laid his ear on Mary's large belly. "You guys alright in there?" Elmo playfully yelled. "You're so silly," Mary said as she kissed Elmo on his forehead. "What kind of kiss was that?" he asked. Mary then grabbed his face and planted a large long kiss on his lips. "Was that better," she asked. Elmo smiled.

Just then the phone rang. "Hello," Elmo answered.

CHAPTER ELEVEN

Meanwhile, Red Beard had gone out for a few beers, leaving Jodi all alone. Jodi decided that now would be a good time to call Elmo and warn him of how treacherous and evil Red Beard was. She waited to be sure that Red Beard really left before she would call. She waited at least ten minutes. Deciding it was now safe to call, she tried to make the phone call twice. The line was busy both times. She started to panic slightly because she feared that Red Beard would come back any minute. So, she decided to write a letter to Elmo. She searched frantically for a pen, pulling everything out of the desk drawers. Finally, she found a pen and a small white tablet without line. She wrote, "Dear Elmo," and gave a brief summary of Red Beard, his actions, personality, and where he could be found. She ended it with, "When you catch this bastard, make sure you kill him or he will kill you!" Then closed it with, "Your friend, Jodi." She hid it under the mattress until the time would become right to mail it to Elmo.

Jodi relaxed. She sat at the dresser and combed her hair. She thought to herself on how sly and cunning she had been all the way from the start. She looked around at the drab, dull painted room. The large long cracks in the ceiling that from an ant's point of view would look like long highways to travel. Jodi then laid across the bed and wondered what would Elmo do to Red Beard. Would he kill him? How? When? Where? The thoughts raced in her mind. She felt no pity for Red Beard. In fact, she would be glad when this is all over because she was getting tired of the whole thing. Jodi fell into a peaceful sleep. About three and a half hours later, Red Beard walked in. He was drunk again, as usual. He stumbled across the room and bumped into the dresser. As he fumbled around to take his clothes off, he fell on the floor with a loud thud. He mumbled something before he fell into a deep sleep. Jodi sighed with relief. She dreaded the thought of having to make love to him. She went to sleep this time being able to have some peace of mind.

Morning came too soon. It was very cold outside and everything was covered with about four inches of snow. The first real accumulation of the winter season. The streets were congested with slow-moving traffic. Automobiles were slipping and sliding as if the drivers had never driven before in the snow. The same drivers that drive every winter, the same way. The holiday season was quickly approaching. People were out early, doing Christmas shopping. Jodi watched out the window as a car pulled up and parked across the street. It was Big Betty and Big Bertha Brown. They were the Brown sisters.

Both were gigantic women with massive bone structures. On their large bodies were what seemed like tons of flesh. They put you in mind of two Chinese sumo wrestlers with red hair. They shuffled into the small apartment, neither bothered to knock. The Brown Sisters were close friends of Red Beard's. They often would act as body guards for Red Beard. Big Bertha opened her purse and pulled out a bottle of whiskey. "Let's get the day started right," she murmured. As she poured four shot glasses clear to the brim with the strong-smelling liquid, Red Beard just moaned and rolled over. The Brown Sisters laughed as they drank a toast to Red Beard. Jodi hesitated before she lifted the glass to her mouth. Thinking to herself that she better go along, she held her breath, took a big swallow and the full glass of whiskey was suddenly empty. Big Bertha again filled the glasses. This time Jodi made the toast.

"Here's to the Red Raiders!" she yelled. "May they live happily drunk and die happily drunk." They all swallowed the liquor and immediately poured more into the glasses. The Brown Sisters, not realizing exactly what Jodi's toast meant, they drank to it anyway. After a few more drinks they became silly acting. Laughing at any and everything. They even laughed at a roach that had just fallen into one of the glasses. There was a small amount of whisky in the glass and as the roach swam in it they became hysterical with laughter. Big Betty said, "He's so lucky, he gets to swim in it. I wish I could swim in it." "Sure," Big Bertha replied, "I'd like to see you put your big ass in that wee glass." They all burst into thunderous laughter as Big Bertha picked up the glass and swallowed the whiskey, roach, and all. They laughed harder.

"What the hell's going on," Red Beard murmured, as he woke up. "Looks like you bitches have started the party without me," he said. "Did you save me any?" he asked. "Sure," Big Bertha answered as she pulled out another bottle. "There's plenty more where that came from," she said. Red Beard didn't even shower or freshen up. He did, however, go to the bathroom to relieve himself. He looked in the mirror at his blood-shot eyes and splashed a handful of cold water in them. "I'm ready," he yelled, as he staggered over to the table and sat down. He had a drink. Then another. It wasn't long and he was as drunk as he was the night before. It was only ten o-clock in the morning.

Soon other members of the Red Raiders arrived and each one brought a bottle of the same brand of whiskey. The small room was now full of red-headed, leather wearing, drunken women. Jodi's blonde hair made her stand out from the crowd but they all accepted her because she was tough and also she was Red Beard's main lady.

About an hour had passed and the drunken women became rowdy. Big Betty and her sister, Big Bertha, stood up in the middle of the room, back to back, and challenged everyone, except Red Beard, to a wrestling match. "We're not that crazy," one of the women yelled. Another yelled, "But we're that drunk!" They all started laughing. Suddenly all eight of the women, including Jodi, leaped on the two big Brown Sisters. What started out as a friendly wrestling match quickly turned into an all out fist fight.

The Brown Sisters were slamming the women all over the place. Women were flying into the walls. As fast as they hit the floor, they were right back in there pounding with both fists. The fight seemed like it lasted for hours, but actually it was over in about five minutes. The room was in shambles. Broken glasses and bottles were everywhere. Furniture was turned over and the one-room bachelor suite was now a one-room big mess. The mattress was even off of the bed. No one noticed, but there lying on the floor was the letter that Jodi had written to Elmo. It laid there, right out in the open. Jodi had walked into the bathroom not noticing the letter on the floor. The others started cleaning up. Sadie Mathews, the woman that Slick Rick would occasionally spend time with, picked up the letter and read it out loud.

Suddenly the room became very quiet as Sadie read the letter. Jodi opened the bathroom door and as she hesitated, looking in the mirror, she could hear Sadie's voice reading the letter. Jodi suddenly closed and locked the bathroom door. She began to panic because she knew she was in big trouble. "Oh my God," she thought to herself, "what am I going to do?"

"Come on out of there bitch," Big Bertha yelled. Jodi didn't know what to do. She was tremendously scared. Sweat beads formed on her face. "Wait a second," she said, stalling for time. "What to do! What to do!" she thought to herself.

Suddenly the bathroom door came crashing down as Big Bertha furiously attacked it. Big Bertha grabbed Jodi by her neck and lifted her straight up into the air.

Holding her there. "Bring the bitch out here," Red Beard thundered. As the large woman marched Jodi into the room, Jodi could see the angry faces staring at her. The blows were so hard that she fell to the floor. "Who in the hell is Elmo?" the big man screamed. Jodi stood up. Her face was red from being hit. Her blonde hair a mess. With one tear in her left eye, she stared at the massive built man. He slapped her again! Then again! "Tie her up!" he hollered.

Two of the women forced Jodi to sit down in a chair. They pulled the sheet off of the bed and wrapped it around Jodi and the chair, tying it tightly. Jodi struggled, but it did no good. Red Beard plugged in an iron and turned it on to as hot as it could get. "Who, and where is Elmo?" he asked. "I don't know" was her answer. Jodi didn't think that Red Beard would hurt her because he loved her so much. Suddenly the hot iron touched Jodi's arm. She screamed loudly! He held it there for what seemed like minutes. Several minutes. When he pulled the iron off of her it left a red spot, the same size as the iron itself. Jodi cried hysterically! "Who is Elmo and what business does he have with me?" Red Beard yelled again.

Jodi didn't answer!

As Red Beard aimed the steaming hot iron towards Jodi's face, she started crying again. She could feel the heat on her face getting hotter and hotter. Her eyebrows started to singe. She closed her eyes and all she could see was red on the inside of her eyelids. "Okay! Okay! I'll talk," she screamed as the pain became unbearable.

Jodi told the whole story. She was so scared and in such pain that she didn't leave out anything. She even told of Slick Rick and how they both were spies for Elmo. Red Beard looked at Jodi and feelings of love for her could be seen in his eyes. He leaned down and kissed Jodi. He then untied her. He hugged her and kissed her again and she answered his kiss with a kiss of her own. They embraced as tears filled his eyes. Suddenly Red Beard snapped Jodi's neck, breaking it. She fell limp in his arms. Red Beard cried!

CHAPTER TWELVE

Across town, Slick Rick was still living the good life. He continued the love affairs with both Faye and Gina. Neither still did not know of the other. Slick Rick had been living up to his nickname, for he was truly a "slick Rick." But little did he know that Red Beard was on to him.

Slick Rick was at Gina's house for dinner and a little love making. He and Gina sat at the dinner table, eating steak and potatoes. Rick was explaining to Gina about his new business venture. He had bought investments, stocks, in a local computer sales company. He also was dealing in real estate sales. He obtained his license and was well on his way to having a legit successful career. They toasted to his career with two freshly poured glasses of champagne.

Slick Rick was becoming more involved with Gina. He was beginning to fall in love with her. He noticed that he spent more time with her than he did with Faye. He liked Faye a lot, but Gina was his love. He was even starting to feel guilty about being with Faye intimately, and taking her money. Slick Rick was becoming sentimental, and he felt good about it.

After dinner, Rick and Gina went straight to bed. They made love and this time it was different. It was more emotional. They both felt the love in the air and they wanted it to last. "I've been thinking," Rick said, "Do you think…." Rick hesitated. "Go ahead, honey," Gina said in her sexiest voice, "I'm listening," she said. Gina gazed unto his eyes. He stared into hers. They kissed a long, hard, emotional kiss. Then Rick took a deep breath and said, "Gina, will you marry me? Will you be my wife?" Gina smiled and said, "I thought you'd never ask! Yes, my love," she answered very nobly. "Yes, I'd love to be your wife." They kissed again.

The next day Slick Rick and Gina made their wedding plans. They were both happy and full of love. Secretly, deeply inside, Slick Rick knew he had some unfinished business to take care of.

Gina left for work. "Why don't you move all of your things in today," she said. "It's time you got out of that motel, don't you think?" she asked as she kissed him good-bye and walked out the door. Gina didn't know that Slick Rick hadn't been staying in a motel. He was really staying with Faye across town.

Slick Rick got dressed and went over to Faye's house. Faye could sense that something was wrong. "Who is she?" Faye asked. Faye had a sad look on her face and she fought back the tears. Slick Rick knew that he had to break it off with her, but he didn't want to hurt her. "Yes, there is someone else," he said reluctantly. "You love her, don't you?" Faye asked. She watched his expressionless face. He felt uncomfortable. "Never mind," she said sternly, "you don't have to say a word because it's written all over your face."

Slick Rick turned and walked out the door. When he reached the door, he stopped and turned around. They stared at each other. "Good-bye," Faye said. He turned and walked out the door, never looking back.

As he drove through the city on the ice covered streets, he didn't realize that Red Beard and his gang was looking for him. He didn't know that Jodi was dead. He didn't know that at that very moment, Red Beard was planning to kill him.

Slick Rick drove over to the West side. He turned off of the freeway onto West Third Street. He stopped at a grocery store on the corner of Third and Broadway. He bought a 40 oz. bottle of Old English 800 malt liquor. He was smack dab in the middle of a black neighborhood. Little black kids were playing on sleds in the middle of the street on Broadway. The yards and sidewalks were litter-filled with wine bottles and trash. Slick Rick sat in his car. As he drank his malt liquor, he noticed a familiar face walking down the street towards his car. It was Bus Coole. "Hey man," Bus called, "let me cop a squat and get some of this heat." Slick Rick nodded for him to get in.

"Have a taste," Slick Rick said, as he shoved the bottle towards Bus. "No thanks, man," Bus said, as he reached in his pocket and pulled out a bottle of Tanguray gin. "As cold as it is, we need some anti-freeze in us to keep us warm." He took a swig of it and said, "I guess you're uptight about Red Beard looking for you, aren't you?" "What?" Slick Rick asked. "Do you mean to tell me that you haven't heard?" "Heard what, man?" Slick Rick asked again. "Aw, man," Bus started to explain, "Red Beard heard somehow that you and Jodi were putting a make on him. He killed Jodi."

"What?!" Slick Rick asked with astonishment and fear in his voice. "Yeah, that's right," Bus added, "and he is supposed to be looking for you." Slick Rick took another drink and it was plain to see that he was becoming nervous. He lit a cigarette and fumbled with it, not even smoking it. He started looking around nervously. "Be cool man," Bus told him. "If I were you, I'd either get out of town or call Elmo and hide out for a few days." "That's what I'll do. I'll call Elmo and let him know what's happening." Slick Rick said, pulling himself together.

Bus shook Slick Rick's hand and hopped out of the car. Slick Rick pulled off and headed home. When he arrived home, Gina wasn't there yet. He tried to call Elmo, but because of the heavy ice and snow, some of the telephone lines were down. He couldn't get through. He tried every ten minutes to no avail. He went to the kitchen and fixed a ham sandwich. He grabbed a cold beer, and slinked to the living room to watch television. As soon as he turned it on, the news was on. Jodi's face appeared. He turned it up as the news reporter told of how Jodi was found in a nearby park with a broken neck. The killer was not found and they had no motives or suspects. Just then Gina came in the door. Slick Rick immediately told her the whole story. Gina automatically became startled and frightened. "What are we going to do?" she asked. "I don't know. As far as I know," he stated, "Red Beard doesn't know about you. He doesn't know where to find me or he would have been here by now. I'll just keep trying to get a hold of Elmo." He then picked up the phone and dialed Elmo's number again. "It's ringing," he said excitedly. He heard Elmo's voice say "Hello."

CHAPTER THIRTEEN

"Hello," Elmo answered. "I finally got you," Slick Rick said with a sigh of relief in his voice. "What's up," Elmo asked. "We've got big trouble," said Slick Rick. "Big trouble," he repeated.

As Slick Rick explained in detail of the happenings, Elmo found it hard to believe his ears. First his little brother dead, and then his good friend, Jodi. And to know that the man that killed them both still lived only sixty-five miles away, as if it never happened. Well, it did happen, and Elmo knew he had to do something about it. He knew that he couldn't, and wouldn't dare go to the police. This is a personal thing, he thought to himself, and he personally would take care of it.

"Okay, Slick Rick," Elmo said, "you've done a great job, man, and I owe you. Give me your number and I'll contact you as soon as I get there, but in the meantime, lay low and keep out of sight." Elmo wrote down the number and said good-bye. He explained to Mary of the conversation as Mary's face was overcome with shock and disbelief.

Elmo and Mary sat quietly, their minds in heavy thought and meditation. They sat there for over an hour, neither saying a word. Elmo broke the silence by saying, "Why don't you go on to bed honey? I'll be in a little later." Mary kissed Elmo and said goodnight. Elmo just sat there in a trance, staring into the carpet. He knew the time was coming to put a stop to Red Beard.

CHAPTER FOURTEEN

A few weeks had passed and it was now Christmas Eve. Snow had fallen and the cold white flakes had covered everything with about 8 inches. By this time, all of Ohio was covered with snow. The city was a beautiful sight of colored lights in every house. Christmas trees were beautifully decorated in every window. The Ohio River and the city skyline was such a gorgeous sight. Christmas carolers were going door to door and their voices singing in perfect harmony could be heard. The sounds of Christmas and the smell of fresh pine were in the air. People hustled into stores doing their last minute shopping.

Elmo sauntered into the "Heavy Metal" Motorcycle Club. It was a black club with maybe one hundred members. He was checked at the door and searched for weapons. As he swaggered over to the bar he noticed that the club was full of people but he didn't know any of them. He nodded to a few familiar faces but there was no conversation. A short good-looking black lady working behind the bar came over to Elmo. "Can I help you," she asked, as she wiped the bar dry with a dishrag. "Cold beer," Elmo answered, "any kind" he said. She brought the beer to Elmo.

As he sat there and sipped on his beer, he looked around to see if there was anyone that he knew. The bar was dark, with lights over the two pool tables, beer signs lit up scattered throughout the bar room. The room to the right of the bar had several tables with chairs and a ladies and men's restroom in two corners of the room. It was filled with smoke above the heads of about twenty to thirty black men and women. Most were dressed in leather coats and blue jeans. Some couples were slow dancing to an old Marvin Gaye song, As Elmo looked into the room to the left, he noticed about another fifteen to twenty couples slow dancing to the same song, piped into the room through a large speaker mounted in a corner, up on the walls and ceiling. There were no tables in this room for it was strictly for dancing. A red and blue light was focused on a dome mirrored ball that moved in a circular motion, making small reflections of colored lights that bounced on the walls and on the couples that held each other tightly as they pushed their pelvises together.

Elmo drank another beer, then left the clubhouse. He drove on the snow covered streets, making his way across town to the north side. When he reached his house and pulled into the driveway, he sat there for a few minutes as he stared at the beautiful and colorful decorations on his house. A big brown sleigh with a Santa Claus in it, led by twelve reindeer, was sitting upon his roof. A large red banner with "Merry Christmas" in white letters hung across the front of the house. The two evergreen trees in the yard and the hedges in front of the house, stretching all the way around to the rear, were covered with red, blue, and green lights. A large Christmas tree, beautifully decorated, was standing in the front picture window.

Elmo smiled as he thought of the past Christmas seasons that he shared with his younger brother Judd. He remembered the time when he and Judd stayed up all night on Christmas Eve so that they could see Santa when he came down the chimney. They had put a glass of milk and several cookies on the table and sat on the couch in their pajamas, waiting for Santa. When they both fell asleep, their mom and dad tip-toed in the room and laid presents all around under the tree. His dad drank the milk and ate the cookies. They quietly went back to bed. About six a.m. that Christmas morning. Elmo and Judd awakened and were very happy to find the presents under the tree and milk and cookies gone. They ran into their parent's bedroom and happily jumped on the bed to wake them up. Elmo remembered how excited young Judd was to open his presents. He remembered that his parents weren't rich but they always had a good Christmas.

Elmo's visions faded in his mind and he decided to go into the house and be with his wife, Mary. On the way into the house, Elmo picked up a few choice pieces of firewood to throw in the fireplace. As he threw the wood on the hot cinders, Mary came into the room. "Hi, honey," she said as she and Elmo kissed. "You've been drinking, haven't you?" she asked. "How did you know?" Elmo asked. Mary held her fingers up to pinch her nose.

"Whew" she said. "Oh, okay, I'll go freshen up," he said, with a chuckle in his voice. Elmo went to the bathroom and ten minutes later, returned with his bathrobe on and sat down in his favorite over-stuffed chair. They talked for a while and watched television. After the eleven o-clock news went off, they went to bed.

About three-thirty a.m., Mary started yelling to wake Elmo up. "I think it's time," she said excitedly. It's time! Elmo jumped up and called the doctor. No more than minutes they were on the way to the hospital. Elmo paced the floor in the waiting room for hours. A nurse entered the room and told Elmo that he may as well go home because it would be quite a while before the babies would be here. Elmo wouldn't go home. Instead, he sat in the lounge chair and went to sleep. About eight-thirty in the morning, a man and his seven year old twin sons walked into the waiting room and as the man instructed the two young boys to sit down and be quiet while he went to see his wife, he left the boys there sitting across the room from the still sleeping Elmo. Suddenly the two inquisitive seven year olds tip-toed over to Elmo and quietly stared directly into Elmo's face. They were only about five inches from his face. Just staring! Suddenly Elmo opened his eyes and thinking that he was dreaming, closed his eyes. After a few seconds, Elmo opened his eyes quickly and let out a scream that scared the little boys. Elmo was just as scared for he thought that this set of twins was his, already grown, staring him in the face. The two boys ran across the room laughing at Elmo.

Just then the nurse came into the room and escorted Elmo down a long hall to a large room off to the right. There, looking through a glass window that was large as the whole wall, Elmo gazed at three babies. All were cute and silently sleeping. He noticed the names on the cribs. The first crib had the name Elmo, Jr.; the next crib had the name Judd; and the next crib had the name Mary. "That's funny," Elmo said, "my two twins are named after me and my little brother," Elmo said with a big smile of contentment on his face, "and it's funny that someone else's kid is named Mary, just like my wife."

Just then another nurse rolled in another baby and parked it beside the three already there. The name on it was blank. There was no name on it. Only a sign of a question mark. This baby was also a girl. Elmo smiled at the four babies. The nurse escorted Elmo into a room to see his wife. She laid in the bed with a sweaty face, but with a big bright smile and a look of relief. Elmo kissed her and told her that he loved her and was very proud of the twins. She looked at him and suddenly realized that Elmo didn't understand. "Elmo," she said, "how do you like the babies?" she asked. "Great," he answered. "Those two kids are beautiful and I'm so proud of you," Elmo said. "No," she said, I mean *all* of the kids." Elmo said, "Yes, honey. Whose ever babies those other two belong to, they are beautiful too." Mary held Elmo's hand and smiled as she said, "Elmo, these other two kids are both girls, and they are ours. We had twin boys and twin girls," she said. "Nurse....nurse!" she yelled. As three nurses came running into the room, they almost tripped over Elmo. For he had fainted again.

Three days later, Elmo took his wife and his new large family home for the first time. It was only a few days from the new year. Elmo and Mary were busy taking care of the babies. They named the fourth girl Sarah. So now Elmo, Jr., Judd, Mary, and Sarah were happy and healthy. Needless to say, Elmo and Mary had their hands full, but they were excited and happy. Elmo took the next week or so off of working on cars so that he could help Mary with the kids. Every once in a while, a few of Mary's female friends would come over and help out by washing diapers and feeding the young ones. Life for the happy couple seemed beautiful. It would get a little hectic once in a while, but for Elmo and Mary it was worth it. They were so very proud of their babies. Surprisingly, all four babies looked identical.

Elmo called Slick Rick to check on him and tell him about his new family. After trying several times, he finally got through to him. Slick Rick was still hiding out and was still safe from Red Beard. Elmo told him to hang in there and he would be making his move on Red Beard in a few more weeks. One of the kids started crying so Elmo told Slick Rick good-bye and ran off to get the baby before it woke up the other three.

The next few weeks went by quickly. Taking care of the babies were more routine now and not as hectic as it was at first. They seemed to be growing fast and sleeping more. Elmo knew it was time to start making plans to do what he knew he had to do. He called a meeting with a few of his close friends and discussed the up and coming event that was bound to happen. Jesse was for anything that Elmo wanted to do. He was ready to just go into Red Beard's territory and blow him away. The more Elmo listened to the other men talk, the more he realized that he was involving more of his friends and he began to feel guilty because he really didn't want to risk their lives. He had already felt bad about losing Jodi. So he secretly planned to do it himself. But he let Jesse and the other men think that they would be involved.

So, as they made plans to ride down on Red Beard, the day, the time, and everything. As they shook hands and the men left, Elmo quickly erased the plans in his mind. He was thinking that he would do as they planned, but he would leave a half day early so he could do it alone. Elmo drank another beer and went into the bedroom to check on the babies. Seeing that the kids were sleeping soundly, he took a shower and joined his wife in bed. He told his wife how he felt bad about involving Jesse and his other friends. Elmo told her of his secret plans. She didn't agree with him and expressed her feelings about it, but Elmo didn't and wouldn't listen. He had his heart and mind set on doing this himself.

Elmo picked up the bedside telephone and called Slick Rick. He told him that he would be there next Saturday night to take care of business. When he hung up the phone Mary laid her head on his chest and sobbed. Elmo reached over and turned out the light and laid there quietly. As Mary sobbed she asked Elmo to think it over before he makes up his mind. Elmo stared at the ceiling, took a deep breath and whispered, "Honey, my mind is already made up."

Mary sobbed as Elmo continued to stare at the ceiling. He reached over and turned on the radio and soft music was playing. He folded his hands behind his head and they both silently fell asleep.

CHAPTER FIFTEEN

The day finally arrived that Elmo planned to seek Red Beard and avenge the death of his little brother. He realized that only sixty-five miles away, in the same state, he would find his mortal enemy. Early that Saturday morning, Elmo played with the kids and with Mary. One could sense the joy and love that Elmo had for his family. Elmo was a true family man in every sense of the word. He was cured now of his overwhelming, quick temper. He was now more settled and tranquil. But Elmo knew that he would have to reach down in the depths of his soul to get mad enough to carry out his revengeful act. This was just something that he knew he had to do. Mary knew it was useless to try to talk Elmo into forgetting about the revenge. She tried several times. But Elmo wasn't having it. He often thought of letting the law handle it, but no way. This was something that he felt was a personal matter and that's all there was to it.

Elmo went out to the garage and started working out. He lifted weights and jogged in place for several hours. After working out, he went back into the house and called his friend, Jesse. He told Jesse to gather about a dozen of the boys and meet him at the clubhouse at 8:00 p.m. He told Jesse to tell them to be prepared for battle.

Elmo hung up the phone and spent the rest of the day playing with the children. He finally put them to sleep and started to get dressed to go get Red Beard. Mary pleaded with him but to no avail. It was 6:00 p.m. Elmo was ready. He loaded his shotgun and his nine millimeter, and put his Bowie knife in a sheath and hung it on his belt. Elmo kissed Mary and his kids and walked out the door. He had planned to leave two hours early alone, so Jesse and the boys wouldn't be involved. As he drove down I-70 Interstate, headed for Dayton, he smiled to himself as he thought that he would pull this over, the revenge, all by himself. He would be able to since he told Jesse to meet him at 8:00 p.m. He had at least a two hour head start on them, so he thought. About 6:30 p.m., Jesse and about twenty bikers went to Elmo's house to surprise Elmo. When they got there, Mary told them that he had left a half hour ago. Jesse and the boys went back to the clubhouse and Elmo wasn't there. Suddenly Jesse realized that Elmo went to Dayton alone. Jesse and the boys loaded into three vans and headed for Dayton. They drove up to ninety-five miles an hour.

Elmo arrived in Dayton and called Slick Rick from the first telephone booth that he saw. Slick Rick told Elmo to meet him at the Roadrunners Clubhouse on South Euclid Street. Twenty minutes later, they were sitting in the clubhouse drinking a beer. Slick Rick was telling Elmo of the whereabouts of Red Beard and the best time to ride down on him. Bus Coole and Trigger walked in and Slick Rick introduced his friends to Elmo. They talked for a while and Wild Dog and Big Frank and several other bikers walked in. Wild Dog, the Roadrunners' president, took a vote from the other bikers and they voted to go with Elmo and stand to fight if they had to.

It was the last day of the month in February and it was surprisingly very warm. A lot of the boys had their bikes, but the majority of them rode in cars. They loaded up their pistols and jumped into cars and on bikes, and they headed across town to Brown Street, where Red Beard and his gang were to be found. Slick Rick, Elmo, Bus Coole, and Wild Dog rode together. They pulled up across the street from the rival gang's clubhouse, with about twenty-five members of the Roadrunners pulling up behind them. Big Frank hollered for Elmo on the C.B. They all had previously agreed to use the Channel 28 for their communication.

"Breaker! Breaker!" Big Frank yelled. Elmo picked up the microphone and said "Talk to me." Big Frank's voice answered from the small black box saying, "It's you baby, Elmo. Whenever you're ready, we are," he said. Elmo pressed on the button and said, "Okay, Big Frank. Send somebody to check to see if Red Beard is in there." A few minutes later, Running Man was out of the car and moving through traffic, crossing the street towards the clubhouse. As he peeked into the side and rear windows of the clubhouse, Elmo could feel the intensity and anger building up inside. He finally would get revenge for his brother. Minutes passed. Suddenly Running

Man reappeared and came swiftly back across the street towards Elmo's car.

"Yes," Running Man said, "Red Beard and about ten of his red-headed bitches are in there." Right then, about twenty more members of Red Beard's gang pulled up on Harley's and parked right in front of the clubhouse. As they dismounted and went inside, one of the bitches, Sadie Matthews, the one that Slick Rick had an affair with, noticed Slick Rick sitting in the car across the street. She stared at him and then suddenly rushed into the clubhouse. Slick Rick knew that she would tell Red Beard, so he urged Elmo to make his move.

As Elmo, Bus Coole, Wild Dog, Big Frank, and all of the others started to walk across the street, Red Beard and his gang burst through the front door and spread out on the sidewalk. They had baseball bats, knives and chains. There was about thirty of them. Four of the red-haired bitches jumped on motorcycles and positioned them in the street, blocking traffic. They pulled two bikes on one side and two on the other, parking them in the middle of the street so the boundaries were set. Traffic was stopped on both sides. People blew horns and yelled. Red Beard motioned to some of his gang members with a wave of his hand and several of them started breaking the windows of the blocked cars with their ball bats. Elmo and his partners watched in disbelief. Red Beard laughed out loud, sounding like a crazy man with a thirst for blood.

Elmo nodded to his partners and all at once they stepped into the middle of the street, between the motorcycles barriers, into the fight zone. Red Beard snapped his fingers and his gang members surrounded Elmo and his partners. Intensity was mounting. Red Beard stood on top of a car and roared madly like a bear and beat his chest like a wild gorilla. The red-headed women started howling like a pack of wild coyotes or wolves.

Elmo and his partners were outnumbered one and a half to one. But they showed no fear. Elmo turned to his partners and said with a loud voice, "Don't touch Red Beard. He's all mine." Suddenly the sounds of tires screeching and doors slamming could be heard behind the already stopped and blocked traffic. Footsteps could be heard running towards the battle zone. Jesse and Elmo's friends from Columbus came running up to Elmo and Jesse slapped a high-five to Elmo. "Let's do it," Jesse said, as he and Elmo smiled at each other. Now Red Beard was outnumbered. A look of worry came on Red Beard's face. Big Bertha yelled at Red Beard and said, "Well, what in the hell are we waiting for!" Red Beard let out another loud roar and then yelled, "Attack!!"

Suddenly both gangs met and clashed. They fought with a tremendous amount of anger. The Brown sisters stood back to back as usual and they fought hard. But even they were no match for Bus Coole and Slick Rick. After a few hard-hitting blows to their heads, the heavy-set Brown sisters were laying on the ground. As they all fought, Red Beard didn't. He continued to stand on top of the car and roar like an animal. But Elmo was fighting and beating each red-headed bitch that he came close to.

The sounds of fists hitting bodies, and bodies hitting the ground with thuds could be heard.

Even though Elmo and his partners had guns, they didn't pull them out. They didn't want to kill anybody unless it was necessary. The fight went on for several minutes. One by one, the red headed gang were falling to the ground. They were literally being whipped down. Finally, all of the Red Raiders gang was laying on the ground, either knocked out or moaning in pain. Elmo had the "look to kill" in his eyes. Red Beard was not afraid, though. Suddenly Red Beard struck Elmo with a chain two times before Elmo finally caught it and wrestled Red Beard to the ground. Elmo hit him fiercely in the face, three times. He then kicked him in the side. As he started to kick again, Red Beard caught his foot and twisted it, sending Elmo whirling hard to the gutter.

Red Beard then pulled out a long knife and viciously cut Elmo across his forehead and again on his left arm. Suddenly, Slick Rick grabbed Red Beard to save Elmo's life and Red Beard turned to Slick Rick and plunged the big knife into Slick Rick's stomach. Slick Rick stumbled backwards and with the look of disbelief in his face, fell to his death. Elmo, seeing what had happened, became furious. He attacked Red Beard and yelled, "Noooooo!!!!" Elmo hit the big, red-bearded, bald-headed man with all the strength that he could muster. Elmo hit him once in the face, knocking him backwards about five feet. Seconds later, Elmo hit him again in the stomach twice, and as Red Beard bent over, Elmo straightened him back up with a vicious upper cut to the face.

As the big man stood there, he let out a loud, insane laughter and just as he did it, Elmo jumped up and kicked him in the mouth. Red Beard fell back into the row of parked motorcycles and they all fell like a stack of dominoes. The smell of gasoline filled the air. Jason lit a cigarette and calmly took a big puff on it and threw the lit cigarette on the heap of motorcycles. The bikes exploded into a large ball of fire. Elmo drug Red Beard out of the fire, and patted the flames out that was burning the big man. He saved the man from burning to death because he wanted to kill him himself.

As he pulled out his gun and placed it to Red Beard's head, he suddenly had a flashback of Mary and his four kids. He knew that they needed him. He also knew that if he killed Red Beard, he would go to jail and never see his family again. So Elmo stood up and put his gun back into his pocket. He then kicked Red Beard in his side. Just then, sirens pulled up and red and blue flashing lights brightened the area. The police ran up and looked at everyone. When seeing Red Beard, the police officer said, "We finally got you this time Red Beard." They picked him up, cuffed him, and took him away. Elmo looked at his friends and said, "Justice is and will be served." He then smiled at everyone and said, "Let's go home."

THE END

The P's

The P
MCC Houston, TX

Shout outs to my biker people that have had some type of impact on my LIFE.

Elwood "Trigger" Lewis
Kenneth "Barron" Seelig (Rick)
Wayne D. May
George Walker
Truman Harris, Jr.
Tom "TJ" Jones
Luther Miller
Albert "AP" Porter
Robert "Bobby" Brown
Sonny Wallace Gooseberry
Richard Trent/ Don Trent
The "P's" of Houston, TX
The Trucons of Houston, TX
The Roots of Houston, TX
The Ground Pounders of Houston, TX
The Roadrunners of Dayton, OH
The Toro's of Columbus/Dayton, OH
The Zulu's of Akron/Cleveland, OH
Bad to the Bone of Dayton, OH
Black Diamonds of Springfield, OH
Rare Blood MC of Springfield/Dayton/Columbus
Street Lords of Houston
The Flames of Columbus
The Posse of Dayton
Angels on Chrome of Akron, OH

RIP – Robert "The Kid" McConnell
RIP – Roy "Storm" Norman
RIP – Donald "DJ" Jackson
RIP – Ronald "Roscoe" Adams
RIP – Doug Porter
RIP – Michael Couts
RIP – Bobby Robinson
RIP – Marcella Portis
RIP – Danny Pearson
RIP – Marcia White
RIP – Jeff Howell
RIP – "Big Joe"

Printed in the United States
by Bookmasters

Printed in the United States
By Bookmasters